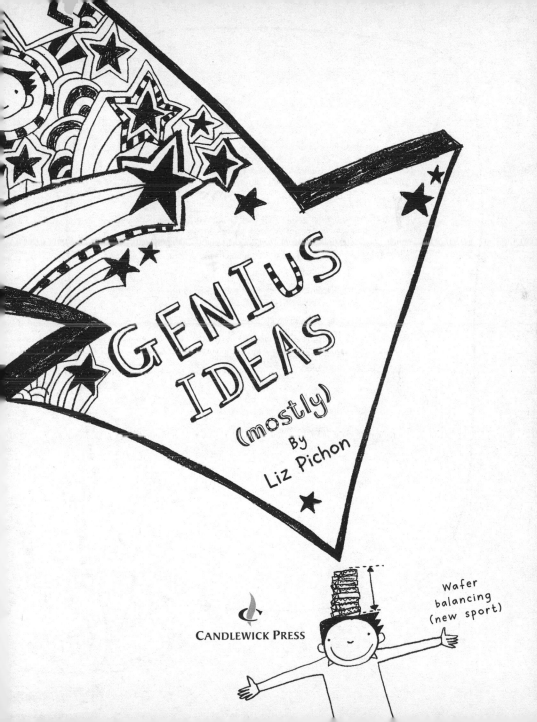

GENIUS IDEAS
(mostly)

By
Liz Pichon

CANDLEWICK PRESS

Wafer balancing
(new sport)

First U.S. edition 2018

Library of Congress Catalog Card Number pending
ISBN 978-1-5362-0129-1

18 19 20 21 22 23 BVG 10 9 8 7 6 5 4 3 2 1

Printed in Berryville, VA, U.S.A.

This book was typeset in Pichon.
The illustrations were done in mixed media.

Candlewick Press
99 Dover Street
Somerville, Massachusetts 02144

visit us at www.candlewick.com

To my sister,

Lyn
xx ♡

Who made me
EXCELLENT toys,
bought lovely
books, and
showed me how
to draw with
fancy pens and
crayons.

Fancy crayons

Beddy
Byes

(This card
was a bit
annoying,
though.)

THIS is a

GENIUS idea...

A FLIP BOOK

in a book. Watch the

bug dance.

So to help me 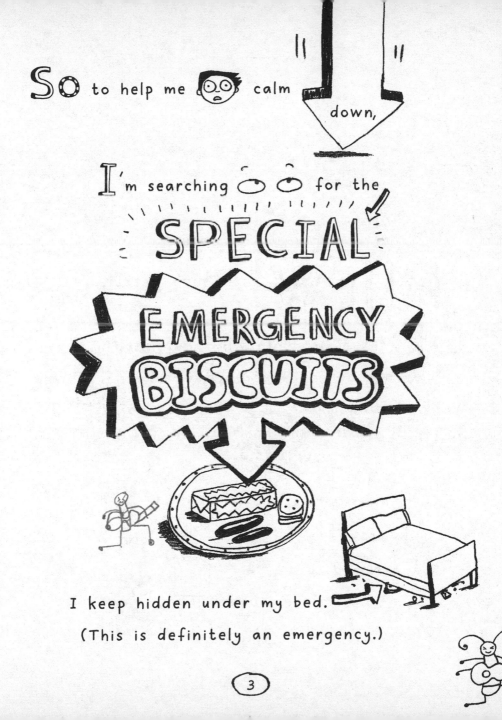 calm down,

I'm searching for the

SPECIAL

EMERGENCY BISCUITS

I keep hidden under my bed.

(This is definitely an emergency.)

biscuit crumbs

PHEW! That's better.

OK, let me explain what happened. I was in the bathroom, pretending to take a shower while reading my comic (like you do), when SOMEONE started KNOCKING really loudly on the door. I assumed it was my sister, Delia ... so I ignored her.

Then she did it again ...

and again ...

and again.

Knock

Knock

Knock

Knock

The **noise** was **very** annoying. But I managed to carry on reading 👁👁 EVERY single page of my comic **REALLY** slowly. **EVENTUALLY** when I'd finished, I very CAREFULLY opened the bathroom door.

I was expecting Delia to SHOUT at me for taking so long. **I** wasn't expecting to see **this.**

It was a HORRIBLE Sight! I let out a LOUD

ARGH!

Which made Dad come running out of the bedroom to see what all the **noise** was about. He said, "What's the problem here?" So I said, "Della's the problem. She **looks SCARY** without her sunglasses!"

Then Dad said it would be **nice** to have just ONE morning without being disturbed by the two of us **ARGUING**.

Delia got REALLY CROSS and pointed at ME, → saying I was the only one who was "DISTURBED." Then she told Dad that he looked

totally ridiculous

before disappearing into the bathroom and

slamming the door.

Which left me in

FULL VIEW

of what Dad was wearing.

I couldn't decide who looked WORSE:

Delia without her sunglasses or Dad in his bike shorts ? Mom wasn't much help either. She came upstairs and

SHOUTED,

"Why is everyone shouting?"

Followed quickly by "And what on EARTH are you wearing?" Dad pointed out that she was the only one who was shouting and the bike shorts were all part of his

Carefully planned new fitness regime.

Which made Mom LAUGH out loud. Ha! Ha! Ha!

I decided that this was probably a good time to head back to my room because:

NASTY SURPRISES + SHOCKS = EMERGENCY BISCUITS.

It's a good thing I keep a few hidden for these kinds of situations. I just hope there are **no more** unwanted surprises today. Sigh ... I eat half of the (second) emergency wafer and start to imagine what MY idea of a *FUN AND VERY RELAXING day at school would be. Mmmmmmm ... I think it would probably go something like this:

Mr. Fullerman is DELIGHTED to see me (even though I'm late).

Hello, Tom, VERY good to see you.

I have my own special **COMFY** chair and table that are as far away as possible from that very annoying **M**arcus **M**eldrew.

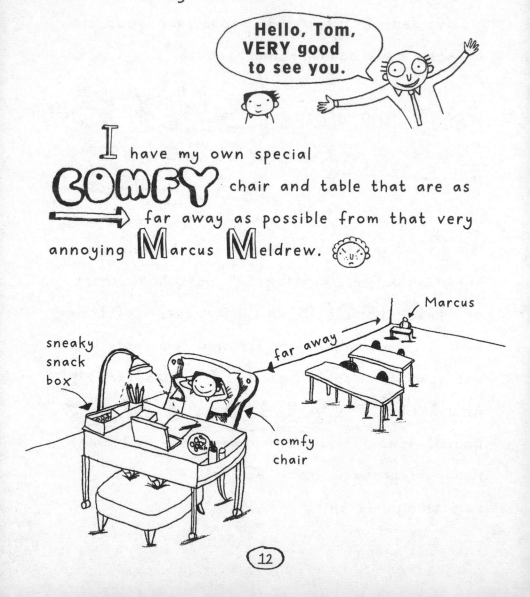

Marcus

sneaky snack box

far away

comfy chair

Lessons are OPTIONAL, so I can choose what I want to do (which is easy).

Choose Your
LESSONS Today

ART	✗
MATH	✓
Doodling	✓
MUSIC	✗
Spelling	
FUN Experiments	✓

Our NICE new art teacher, Miss Straw, insists I do a WHOLE art project on ...

CARAMEL

WAFERS.

Really? If you insist. I have *fun* arranging them into towers before spending as MUCH time as I want drawing and doodling.

Sigh.

Miss Straw is VERY impressed

Well done, Tom!

and lets me eat TWO wafers for my snack.

AND I'm allowed to unwrap the others and use the foil for my interesting wafer collage.

(The wafers I can save to eat later.)

Miss Straw thinks I am an ART BISCUIT GeNiuS.

I agree.

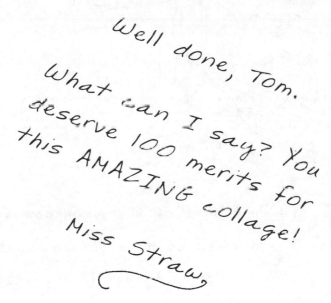

Well done, Tom.

What can I say? You deserve 100 merits for this AMAZING collage!

Miss Straw,

(I show my 100 merits to Marcus, which annoys him.)

Then the day gets even better. A few friends and I have a DELICIOUS lunch served by ...

the teachers.

More ice water, Tom?

TEACHERS' TABLE

I eat in the best part of the lunchroom (for a change). I'm allowed to have SECONDS of pudding, followed by a relaxing rest with my feet up before the next lesson starts.

Which is

EXTRA FUN EXPERIMENTS.

(Outside – because it would be SUNNY ☼ on my perfect day.)

The whole class helps me place hundreds of WAFERS in a **l o n g** row around the school. Then I get to ⟶ *PUSH* the first wafer forward, causing them all to fall one by one in an ⟩AMAZING⟨ pattern

(like dominoes).

Solid

Amy Porter

The **SpeCTAcuLAR** [WAFER] **DISPLAY** breaks the **WORLD BISCUIT FALLING RECORD!**

YEAH!

(And everyone gets to eat a few more of them too.)

Then as a **special** treat, **M**r. Fullerman announces that our **MUSIC LESSON** today will be taught by...

DUDE 3, only the **BEST BAND** EVER! Who arrive at our school in their fancy **↕HUGE** tour bus. They put on a fantastic concert for the entire school, and because Derek (my best mate) and I are **DUDE 3**'s **BIGGEST** fans, we get to stand on stage and play along with our own guitars to all the songs that we know. **DUDE 3** congratulates **US** on how good **WE** are. Which makes **M**arcus make a face like this: Huh?

But that's NOTHING...

compared to the LOOK on Delia's face

when DUDE3 pulls up outside

OUR house in their tour bus.

Then me and Derek

get out, saying, Later, Dude3

to the whole band,

who wave back.

Then we carry our BRAND-
NEW COOL guitars that the band has

given us back to the house.

Now THAT'S MY idea of the BEST and MOST AMAZING DAY at school EVER!

Oh, well ... You never know. Today might turn out to be a GOOD day after all? Like LAST WEEK in the assembly (which I wasn't looking forward to), Mrs. Nap asked everyone a question.

> Who can tell me what month it is and what year?

Before I could put UP my hand to answer, Marcus Meldrew practically LEAPT off the floor, waving his arm around so Mrs. Nap would pick him. She did. But the REALLY funny bit was when Mrs. Nap asked Marcus to sit down and he accidentally said LOUDLY

> Yes, Mommy.

Then he couldn't understand why we were all LAUGHING 😊 so much. Mrs. Nap had to say,

> I think you meant to say,
> YES, Mrs. Nap.

It was HILARIOUS! I laughed a LOT that day. Right NOW, though, if Mom and Dad find out how late I am, I'll be in trouble. Although I'm not sure they'd notice. I can still hear Mom chuckling EVERY time she says the words fitness regime like it's the FUNNIEST joke she's EVER heard.

I'm not laughing because I know that:

DAD + FITNESS REGIME = LOADS MORE DODGY SPORTS OUTFITS. FIT

There's a good chance that he could start turning up at my school, or WORSE STILL, my friends' houses, wearing something EVEN more embarrassing than those BRIGHT BLUE BIKE SHORTS.

IF THAT'S POSSIBLE?

I slip downstairs and grab some breakfast and realize that I am <u>properly late for school</u> now. Mom is upstairs and still a bit busy.

I could go and ask her to write me a nice

LATE NOTE

to give to

Ha! Ha!

(Mom being busy)

Mr. Fullerman, which would probably stop me from getting into any trouble?

OK, TOM

But why bother when it's SO much easier . . .

just to write ✎ ∿∿ one myself.

(A genius idea.)

Dear Mr. Fullerman,

Poor Tom has had a VERY nasty shock this morning due to his ~~rotten stupid~~ sister scaring him. I'm very sorry he's late for school. His sister has been warned not to scare him again (or else).

Because of his SHOCK, Tom might find it hard to concentrate on any tricky math lessons today. Just letting you know.

Thank you,

Rita Gates

There, all done!
(Hopefully **Mr.** **F**ullerman won't suspect
anything dodgy about my note. I didn't mention
Dad's shorts, as that would take too long
to explain.)
Dad comes downstairs and starts doing some
weird kinds of **stretching**
moves.   Mom is SHOUTING from

upstairs to me:

Have you left yet,
Tom?

So I say BYE to Dad quickly and remind him
I might be going to Norman's house for band
practice tonight. He says, "Norman's house
isn't too far. How about I **run** over and
get you?" And I say,

"NO WAY!"

just that little bit too quickly in case he
decides to turn up looking like ...

well, like that.

I tell him Derek's dad is coming to pick us up.

"All sorted, no need to worry, Dad."

Good thinking ...
phew!

I'm here!

Shame

Derek's not waiting outside: he's already left for school. So I set off with my SPECIAL LATE NOTE safely in my bag.

As I walk past the shop, I'm thinking maybe I could POP in for a small snack? (Good idea.) It takes me a while to choose what to have. But because I have a LATE NOTE, I'm hoping Mr. Fullerman will read it and say, **That's all fine, Tom** then let me off the hook.

Mmmmm?

FRUIT CHews

And if he doesn't, at least I'll have my snack to eat.

Fingers crossed.

When I finally arrive at school, no one is around. It's **REALLY** quiet **EVERYWHERE.** Apart from Mrs. Nap's classroom, where I can hear some **odd** noises **W A F t i n g** out of her slightly open door.

It sounds a bit like ...

CATS YOWLING IN PAIN

Owww {w} w'w

Awwwwww

I go and take a sneaky 👁 👁 peek
to see what's going on.

It is Mrs. Nap.

She seems to be Singing

the WHOLE attendance book?

Worse than that, Mrs. Nap is making
the class sing their names back to her.
One by one. Which is PAINFUL
to hear.

Charlie Smith?

Charlie Smith
is here,
Mrs. Nap.

Mrs. Nap is being her usual
cheerful self when she sings.

"Isn't this **FUN**, everyone?"

And Charlie Smith (who's just sung his name) sings back, "NOOOOO, not really."

Which makes **Mrs. Nap** a bit **CROSS**. **So** she sings, "Oh, dear...let's sing it again from the beginning and this time we'll ALL do it properly."

Charlie Smith tries to sing, "I was only joking, Mrs. Nap!" But it's too late.

Luckily for me (and my class) Mr. Fullerman doesn't do "attendance singing." I think we'd be there ALL day if he did.

I'm SO busy peering in the classroom that I don't hear Mrs. Mumble behind me until she says,

> Hello, Tom.

Which makes me JUMP.

"Shouldn't you be in class?"

I explain I was on the way there and I have a LATE NOTE. → SPECIAL Mrs. Mumble remembers there's a "special buddy talk this morning. Mr. Fullerman was taking your class to meet some of the younger children."

So I say, "Great."

And I'm about to go off and find them.

Then she adds, "But I'm not sure WHICH class they've gone to. Best you wait in the school office with me until they're back so I can mark ✓ you present. We don't want you just wandering around school, do we?"

(Me wandering)

I'm thinking . . .

1. What IS a "buddy talk"?

2. How long will I have to sit in the school office, as it can be a *BIT* awkward?

What are you doing here, Tom?

34

Mrs. Mumble points to a seat and asks me
not to talk while she makes an announcement
over the loudspeaker.
At least this should be
fun to watch.

Mrs. Mumble clears her throat
and LEANS into the speaker
while pushing a special RED button.
As soon as she starts speaking, her voice
goes all, well...

Mumbly.

"Attention, OAKFIELD School, can I remind EVERYONE that this Friday it's **Teacher Training Day**, so school will be finished **ONE HOUR** earlier than usual."

I can just about 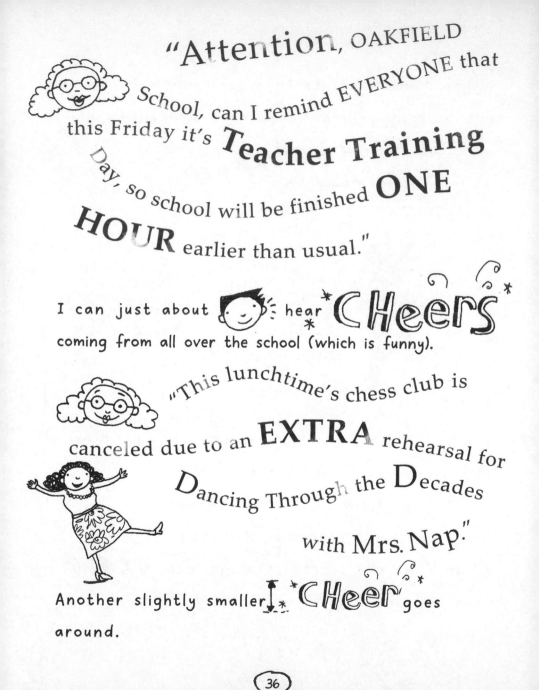 hear *CHeers*

coming from all over the school (which is funny).

"This lunchtime's chess club is canceled due to an **EXTRA** rehearsal for **D**ancing Through the **D**ecades with Mrs. Nap."

Another slightly smaller *CHeer* goes around.

Then she finishes by telling everyone, "One more thing. When Mr. Fullerman returns to his class, could he send someone to collect **TOM GATES** from the school office, as he was **LATE** for school and is waiting in the office to be **COLLECTED**. Thank you."

huh?

GREAT, now the <u>WHOLE</u> school knows I'm late. **AND** Mrs. Mumble has made me sound like I'm some kind of **PACKAGE**.

(Groan.)

TOM GATES
(For collection)
THIS WAY UP

As Mrs. Mumble's finished her message, I MUST remind her about my LATE NOTE so I don't get into trouble.

I say, "Mrs. Mumble, I know I'm LATE but I have a NOTE to explain why."

And she says, "That's good, Tom. I'd like to SEE that note."

Which makes me PANIC a bit.

My note is stuffed into my bag and I can't find it anywhere.

I put my bag **down** onto her desk
so I can **rummage** around.
While I'm looking, I carefully explain
ALL about my **OLDER** sister, Delia,
and how she gave me a **NASTY SHOCK**
this morning (which is true, she did). But I
don't say what happened. **I**nstead I re-create
my **"I'M SHOCKED!"** face like this...

Which startles

Mrs. Mumble a bit.

And because I STILL

can't find my note, I

continue...

39

"It's in here somewhere."

Then I tell Mrs. Mumble how Mom was a bit worried about me because I looked slightly PALE.

"Mom told me I was CLAMMY from the SHOCK and I needed to sit down and recover a bit before going to school. Which is why I'm late, Mrs. Mumble." I do a slightly different type of face ... like this.

Then breathe a SIGH of relief, as I've just found my note. I give it to Mrs. Mumble, who's about to read it when there's a KNOCK at the office door.

LATE note

Hello!

It's **AMY PORTER** from my class. She tells Mrs. Mumble TWO things.

1. I can come back to class, as Mr. Fullerman is there now.

I'm back.

2. The **WHOLE** school has just heard my (why I'm LATE) explanation because the

LOUDSPEAKER is still on.

IT IS?

Mrs. Mumble LIFTS my bag off the SPECIAL red button and says,

"Oh, dear. That'll be why."

I'm doing a "VERY embarrassed" face, which looks like this.

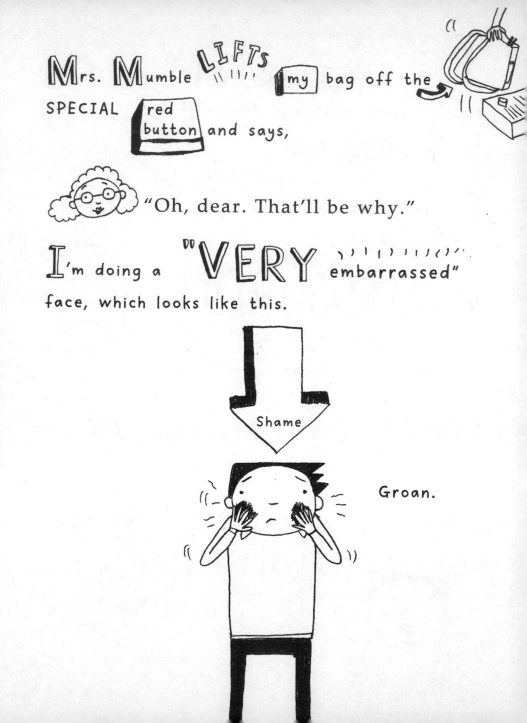

Shame

Groan.

And if that's not bad enough, Mrs. Mumble only goes and brings out her She says, "That reminds me, Tom — I need a picture of you." I say, "RIGHT NOW?" Because I can feel my face going even

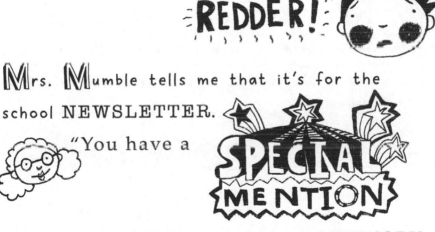

REDDER!

Mrs. Mumble tells me that it's for the school NEWSLETTER. "You have a SPECIAL MENTION

for the EXCELLENT DRAWING HOMEWORK on your school book. Nothing to be embarrassed about, Tom!"

Which **cheers** me up a bit. **I**'d forgotten about being in the NEWSLETTER.

At least **AMY** will see that I don't make stupid mistakes like this *all* the time. Speaking of stupid mistakes ...

Mrs. **M**umble is just about to take the photo when someone else **knocks** at the door. There's a kid standing outside with a COMB STUCK in his hair.

Mrs. Mumble looks at him and says, "How did you do that?"

The kid says he's not really sure.

Mrs. Mumble tells him to Wait there, then goes ahead and takes what I hope will be a VERY Nice picture of me for the NEWSLETTER.

SMILE

Now Mrs. Mumble's got this kid with a comb stuck in his hair to deal with, my LATE NOTE seems to have **slipped** her notice, which is a

BIG RELIEF.
Phew

On the way back to class, **AMY PORTER** wants to know exactly what Delia did that gave me such a **SHOCK.** I _can't_ say "She took off her sunglasses, it was terrible" because **that** doesn't sound shocking at all. (Even though it was.)

Instead I say, "**It** was nothing. I'm over it now." (Like I'm being brave.)

Then I manage to quickly change the subject by asking AMY what the BUDDY TALK was all about.

AMY says the YOUNGER kids get to choose an older kid (one of us) to be their BUDDY. ☺

"We have to look out for them and make sure they're happy in school. That kind of thing. Mr. Fullerman took us to say hello so the little kids know who we all are now." I say, "Lucky them." ☺

Since I wasn't there, I ask **AMY** what happens if you don't get chosen to be a buddy. **AMY** tells me,

"Not <u>all</u> the little kids want to have buddies. So don't worry, it will be less hassle for you not to be picked."

But I think I'd make a good **BUDDY**. I could show them all kinds of really **important** stuff, like:

○ How to be **first** in the lunch line.

sneaky shortcuts

Oh, yes!

Back in class, Mr. Fullerman says,

Better late than NEVER, Tom.

I don't have to explain where I've been because **everyone** has already heard. (Groan.)

Marcus Meldrew can't **WAIT** to tell me how **STUPID** I sounded over the *loudspeaker.*

You sounded stupid.

So I tell him,

"You don't need a LOUDSPEAKER to SOUND **STUPID**."

And he says, "No one will pick you as a buddy because you weren't there."

So I think quickly and say, "No one will pick YOU as a buddy because you WERE there."

Then Mr. Fullerman GLARES at both of us and says,

STOP TALKING.

Which shuts Marcus up ... for now.

Mr. Fullerman says today he's going to read us a story. (I'm hoping this means we'll have a nice RELAXing day after all?)

Then he adds ...

"**Listen** carefully, as we'll be doing some work about the story later."

Mr. Fullerman holds up a book and asks if anyone has heard of

(Groan ...)

Aesop's Fables?

Aesop's Fables

The BOY WHO CRIED WOLF

WOLF

That's me

Boy

And Mark Clump, who hardly EVER puts his hand up, gets VERY EXCITED and says,

Mr. Fullerman, I HAVE, I HAVE. They're my favorite. ☺

Mr. Fullerman asks Mark,

Which is your FAVORITE FABLE, Mark?

And Mark Clump thinks for a while....
(Quite a long while, actually.)
Mr. Fullerman looks impressed that Mark is thinking about his answer SO carefully.

Until he says ...

Plain if it's t(O)asted with butter

and jam ... yum.

Which isn't quite the answer
Mr. Fullerman was expecting.

The class starts LAUGHING Ha! Ha! Ha! Ha! Ha!
because we've just realized Mark thinks
Mr. Fullerman said BAGEL.

Whoops.

So just to make it clear for everyone,
Mr. Fullerman says,

The FABLE —
NOT BAGEL, FABLE —
I'll be reading is called
"THE BOY WHO CRIED WOLF."

Marcus nudges me and says he knows this
story already.

The wolf eats the boy in the
end ... that's it, really.

Thanks for telling me the
ending, Marcus.

That's just great.

The good news is Marcus has given me an idea for a doodle. I carefully arrange a few innocent-looking books on my desk.

While Mr. Fullerman is reading out the story, I get busy drawing.

AMY is watching and smiling. I have to keep stopping to pay attention to Mr. Fullerman.

(Me paying attention.)

Marcus has been ignoring me. Until right at the end of my drawing, when I do a picture of him ...

that catches his eye.

Marcus has only gone and put his hand **UP** and interrupted **M**r. **F**ullerman, who's not very happy. ((

He tells **M**r. **F**ullerman,

"Sir! Tom Gates is drawing, **SIR."**

Luckily for me, **M**r. **F**ullerman doesn't tell me off. I just have to put down my pen and **LISTEN.**

Which I do (for a while).

But Marcus is still watching me. Which is annoying.

So I start to draw this line

Hey↓
Marcus ⟹ Yes, YOU. Follow this line

Don't stop looking!

Keep watching

this LINE, YOU are

If you are

following

STILL

AN ÌDIOT!

Ha!

Ha!

Ha!

Ha!

Ha!

Marcus looks like this now.

(I should try this trick

on Delia too!)

Break Time (at LAST)

My best mate, Derek, ➡ comes to find me. He can't come to band practice tonight, which is a shame.

"I have to go to Aunt Julia's house with my mom." Derek looks really fed up.

"I hope she doesn't do that face-**squeeze** thing on me again. It's embarrassing."

Look at you!

← Aunt Julia

To make Derek feel better, I tell him about when my **A**untie Alice, **U**ncle Kevin, and the cousins came around for a family barbecue last weekend.

Derek says, "I **LOVE** barbecues."
And I say, "**SO** do I, usually."

I explain to Derek,

"It would have been OK, but Dad was in a **REALLY BAD** mood, mostly because of Uncle Kevin and his dodgy **jokes.**

Eating for two?

AND he didn't like my paper banger either, or the **noise** it made. Then when Dad dropped all the sausages on the ground, he said it was **MY** fault!"

(67)

Derek says, "I was wondering where Rooster got those sausages from. **And** what's a paper banger*?"

I still have a paper banger **Scrunched** up in my pocket. So I take it out and try to smooth out the creases to make it work better. It's not great, but it does the trick.

I tell Derek, "I was only showing the cousins how to make it go **BANG!** Like this... by flicking it over my head..."

BANG

*Go to the end of the book for how to make a paper banger.

$\mathbb{D}$erek seems to have cheered up a bit and wants to have a go at making the paper banger work himself.

It takes a few tries,

duff

but eventually Derek gets it at the right angle...

Bang!

to make a very loud

BANG!

The noise attracts a bit of attention from some of the little kids in school, who come over and want to know

What's that?

"It's a paper banger," I tell them. "Look." Then I show them how it works. "You can make them yourself — it's easy."

BANG!

This kid named **Joey** wants to take a closer look. **H**e's the one I saw in the school office with the comb stuck in his hair (which is out now).

I'm very nice and let **Joey** try. I show him the knack of making the banger work properly too. **W**hich is a mistake...

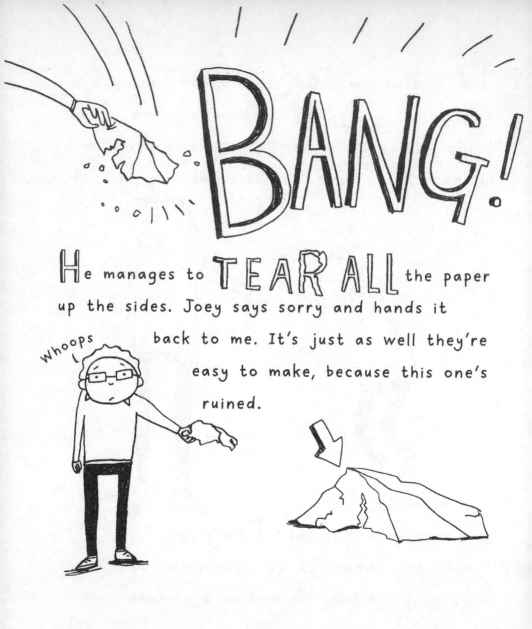

BANG!

He manages to **TEAR ALL** the paper up the sides. Joey says sorry and hands it back to me. It's just as well they're easy to make, because this one's ruined.

Whoops

Derek says **Joey** reminds him of our mate **N**orman when he breaks stuff. **M**ind you, ever since **N**orman fell off his bike and hurt his elbows, he's been a bit more careful about everything he does.

Mind that banana skin.

Derek reminds me to tell Norman that we'll have to cancel band practice tonight. He suggests, "We could do it during the weekend instead?" **A**nd then he says **AGAIN**, "You won't forget to tell Norman, will you, Tom?" And I say, As if!

P.E.

(Stands for Physical Education, or in Norman's case, Poorly Elbows.)

Even though Norman is the FIRST person I see when I come into class, I completely forget to tell him about band practice. Norman gets to miss P.E. because of his elbows.

I ask him if he's being allowed to relax for a bit or do something else? Norman points to some worksheets and tells me, "Mr. Fullerman wants me to catch up with these. He says the class has done them already."

We have?

I take a quick look, but I don't remember doing **ANY** of these worksheets? I'll keep quiet and won't mention it in case Mr. Fullerman wants me to catch up as well.

Tom!

Norman has to go and sit in the **school office** with Mrs. Mumble

Ready, Norman?

(Groan.)

(like I did), while the rest of class 5F follows Mr. Fullerman for P.E.

Follow me!

We get changed and go outside to the playing fields, as the weather is nice and

WARM.

Mr. **F**ullerman announces to the class that we're about to have

LOTS of FUN!

And we all cheer! "**YEAHHH!**"

Then he adds,

Training for our SPORTs DAY!

Which makes us go ...
"Awwwwwwwwwwww."

Training doesn't sound like much fun to me?

Mr. Fullerman tells us to **Warm Up**
by running around the field ➔ once.

Solid (who's not keen on running)
puts up his hand and says,
"Mr. Fullerman, I am really
WARM already, so do I
have to run?"

I think Solid has made a
VERY good point.

So I say, "Sir, I'm VERY WARM too. Phew!"

In the hope Mr. Fullerman might change his mind about making us do all that running.

NO chance.

Mr. Fullerman says,

TWICE around the playing fields for EVERYONE.

Ignoring both of us.

The whole class is GROANING now and staring at us. Apart from Brad Galloway, who loves running. Yes!

Florence Mitchell's not happy.

She says,

Nice work, Tom.

Whoops.

Like it's ALL MY FAULT!

Mr. Fullerman is keeping his BEADY EYES on ME the WHOLE time I'm running. I can't even hide behind a TREE or pretend to be doing up my shoelaces for a quick REST without him shouting,

"Keep going, TOM.... I can SEE YOU!"

I'm REALLY HOT and I've gone BRIGHT RED now.

Solid can hardly SPEAK he's

so TIRED out.

He (just about) says,

"We've ... hardly ... started ... yet."

Which is true. (Groan.)

Marcus Meldrew comes over to ME

and starts waving his " " hands

around my head. (Which is annoying.)

I say, "What are you doing, Marcus?"

And he says,

"My hands are COLD. I'm just warming them up...
ON YOUR FACE!"

Ha! Ha! HA! HA!

Marcus thinks he's HILARIOUS.

I think it's going to be a VERY long P.E. lesson.

Groan.

My class, 5F, has never (I repeat) NEVER won ANYTHING on SPORTS DAY. We're a bit rubbish compared to some of the other classes.

Every year at the end of SPORTS DAY, Mr. Fullerman says,

"WELL DONE, Class 5F. You've ALL done SO WELL! Just remember, it's the taking part that counts."

(Even though we've come in last.)

While Mr. Sprocket's class, Class 5S, is usually

✶ Celebrating ✶...

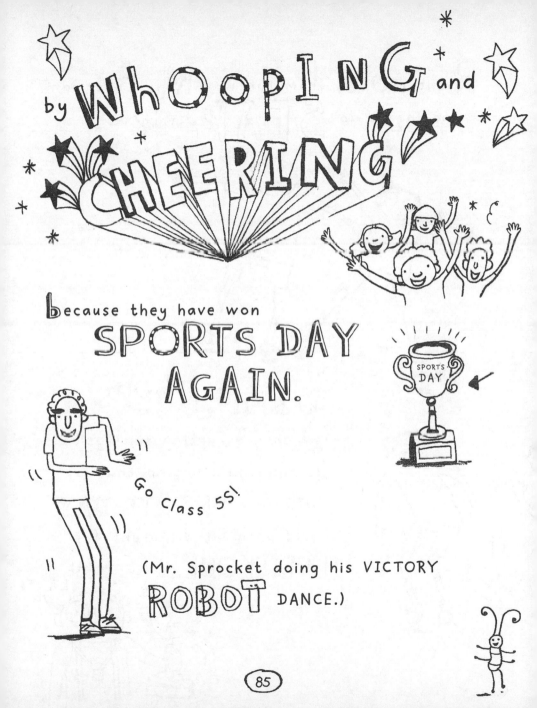

by WHOOPING and CHEERING

because they have won

SPORTS DAY AGAIN.

Go Class 5S!

(Mr. Sprocket doing his VICTORY ROBOT DANCE.)

Right now, from the way Mr. Fullerman is making us do STAR JUMPS

and bunny hops (which are hurting my legs), I think he's hoping that THIS time SPORTS DAY could be a bit different for EVERYONE.

At LAST!

SPORTS DAY

Sometimes I wonder why SPORTS DAY is actually called SPORTS DAY. I'm not sure EVERYTHING we do is a REAL sport?

Like ...

Hula-Hooping

Which is a LOT harder than it looks.

Jumping Rope

Mr. Fullerman says boxers jump rope to keep fit. But they probably don't have someone like Marcus standing RIGHT NEXT to them messing up THEIR jump rope all the time.

Beanbag juggling

BEANBAGS get used a LOT on SPORTS DAY:

we do loads of throwing and catching

and running in between them.

My personal favorite is beanbag balancing.
It's fun to put them on your ___ arms,
knees, or do a double balance on your

knee

and

foot at the same time.

I often pile them on my

head. Mr. Fullerman tells me to

stop when I get to about here.

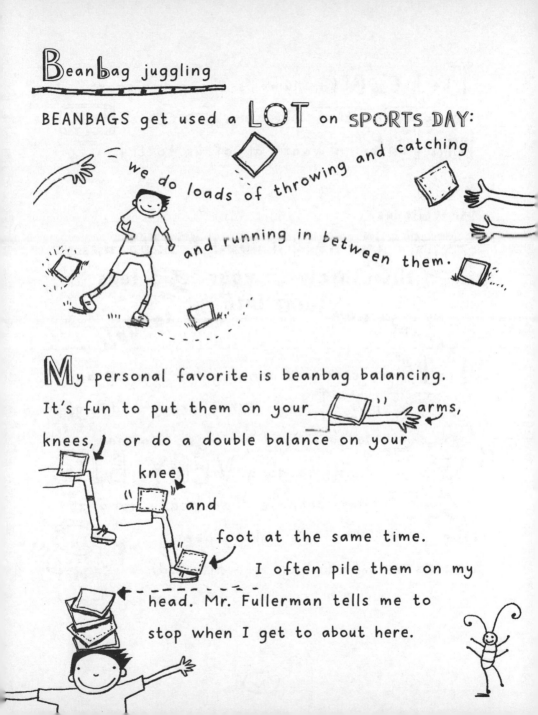

The LONG jump is the only "sport" we do today that I've seen on telly. Mr. Fullerman wants all of us to try.

He tells us, "You need a good *run* up, then throw your legs forward and jump into the sandpit."

Marcus starts bending his legs up and down. I say, "What are you doing, Marcus?" and he says, "I'm getting ready to do a VERY BIG jump, because I am really good at long jump." Now he's taking deep breaths as well (which is a bit odd).

Solid says to me, "Maybe he is good at long jump after all?"

I say, "Let's see."

We watch Marcus as he starts to **RUN** as fast as he possibly can toward the sandpit....

Then he LEAPS into the air and does a really, really...

small jump.

OOOOFFFFF

Mr. Fullerman says,

Good try, Marcus. Stretch your legs out next time.

Now Marcus thinks he's done a BRILLIANT jump.

(He hasn't.)

Mr. Fullerman finishes off our training session with what he says is a COOL DOWN.

Solid says the cool down is making him even HOTTER.

On the way back to school, I can hear Marcus telling ANYONE who'll listen that he is a natural at long jump. (He's not.)

Brad Galloway is doing that funny thing when you walk behind someone really closely and they don't know you're there. He's right behind Solid, copying everything he does. Solid doesn't notice for ages, until I tell him. He says, Good joke, Brad and wants to try it on someone else now.

Trouble is, Solid's a bit **TALL** and **noisy** and his shadow keeps giving him away.

> I know you're there, Solid.

> Hello, Solid.

When we get back to school, Mr. Fullerman asks us to help put away the "sports equipment" (I think he means the beanbags, Hula-Hoops, and jump ropes).

Then he takes the opportunity to remind us how little time there is before SPORTS DAY.

Like we didn't already know.

He says,

> **Team 5F, you are all going to do AMAZINGLY well this year, I can tell...**

Blah blah blah

But it's hard to concentrate when I can see THIS. ➡️

Brad is going crazy behind Mr. Fullerman's back.

I'm trying not to laugh, but it's almost impossible! Everyone who can see Brad dancing starts laughing too.

Mr. Fullerman gets a bit cross and says,

"This is NO laughing matter, Class 5F!"

Ha! Ha!

Ha!

Ha!

Ha!

Ha!

Ha!

Ha! Ha!

Ha!

Because he can sense something is going on behind his back. Then Mr. Fullerman spins around SUPER FAST, just in time to catch Brad Galloway...

97

doing absolutely **nothing.**

(Lucky escape or what?)

Mr. Fullerman says, **"I'll be keeping a close eye on YOU, Brad."**

Which is excellent news for <u>ME</u>, because (in between doing some work) I've been trying to finish my SUPER LARGE doodle

in class.
Which is tricky to
do with

Mr. **F**ullerman
STARING at me
(like he does).

Tom, stop doodling.

Brad, stop dancing.

I can't WAIT until lunchtime to catch up with Norman and Derek and tell them ALL about how BRAD was dancing behind Mr. Fullerman's back.

In the lunchroom, I stand up to show them EXACTLY what he did. Like this: I am very busy WAFTING my arms around over my head and from side to *side*, re-creating Brad's dance. I don't even NOTICE that DEREK is making a funny face at me.

I carry on and say, "Trust me ... it was REALLY funny! Especially when Mr. Fullerman was going ON and ON about SPORTS DAY and Brad Galloway was wobbling his legs around like this...."

Then I tell them that the **BEST** part of all was that Mr. Fullerman had ABSOLUTELY NO idea what Brad was doing behind his back.

Derek nudges me and says,

"I think he does now."

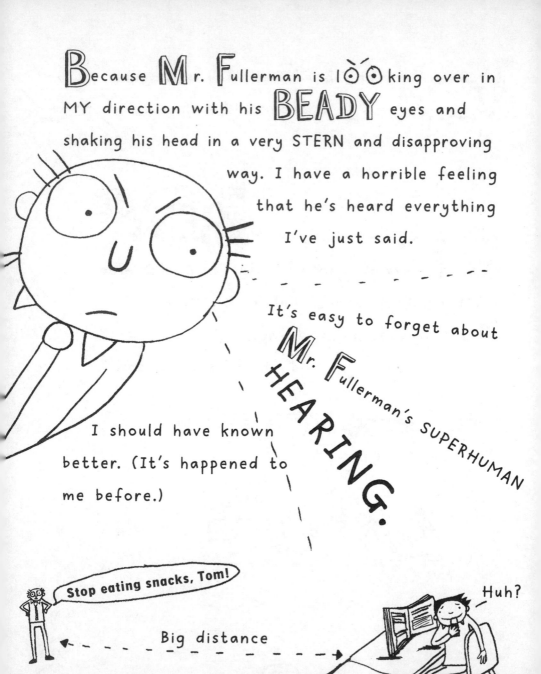

Because Mr. Fullerman is looking over in MY direction with his BEADY eyes and shaking his head in a very STERN and disapproving way. I have a horrible feeling that he's heard everything I've just said.

It's easy to forget about Mr. Fullerman's SUPERHUMAN HEARING.

I should have known better. (It's happened to me before.)

Stop eating snacks, Tom!

Huh?

Big distance

Norman says, "He's still looking."

I try to **focus REALLY** hard on my lunch and whisper,

"Tell me when he's stopped."

Then two VERY important questions suddenly POP into my head.

Question 1. Will Brad get into trouble because of me?

Question 2. Are those REALLY chips on top of my cake?

Answer 1. Mmmmm, possibly?

Answer 2. Yes, they are really chips because Granny Mavis has been cooking again.

I manage to carefully pick out the chips and eat the cake (the two don't usually go together unless you're Granny Mavis). Norman seems keen to eat my chips, which is fine by me (but a bit weird).

Yum.

Then while he's eating, I ask Norman what it was like missing P.E. and having to do his work in the school office. And he says it was all right. But he did find out something interesting. And Derek and I both say, WHAT'S that?

Norman tells us that he overheard a conversation in Mr. Keen's office with Mrs. Mumble.

Chips

He says, "They were both talking about **BANDS**."

"Really?"

Norman continues, "I was being very quiet and not moving around much so I could listen. I heard Mr. Keen say,

Norman
NOT moving

"If we can get **DUDE 3** to play for the school, that would be GREAT. The children would enjoy seeing them."

And I say,

"Are you sure?" And Norman says with a mouthful of chips,

Yes, I'm sure.

Derek wonders why **DUDE 3** would want to play at OUR school? If it DOES turn out that **DUDE 3** is playing in our school, that would be ...

BRILL
AMAZ
FANTAST

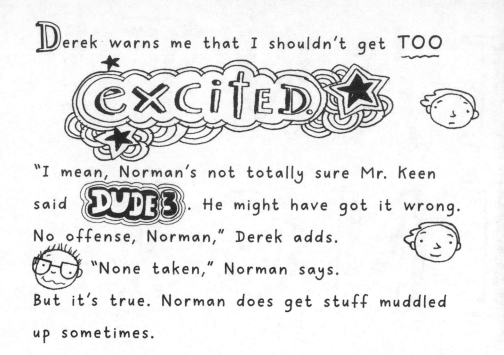

Derek warns me that I shouldn't get TOO

excited.

"I mean, Norman's not totally sure Mr. Keen said **DUDE 3**. He might have got it wrong. No offense, Norman," Derek adds.

"None taken," Norman says.

But it's true. Norman does get stuff muddled up sometimes.

Oh?

TOY HEN →

I said bring a PEN, Norman.

We're getting ready to leave the lunchroom
when we hear a MASSIVE

CRASH!

It's a BIG vegetable accident

with a WHOLE tray of PEAS

being spilled all over the floor.

We're trying to see exactly what happened.

Looks like it was that kid Joey (the one who broke my paper banger).

He's accidentally BUMPED into someone who was carrying the peas.

I can hear Janitor Stan's keys jingling in the distance already as he dashes to the lunchroom ...

squashed peas

with a SUPER large BROOM
to get the peas under control.

(Which is proving very difficult to do.)

We leave Stan swishing his broom around with
a LONG trail of squashed peas behind us.

Mr. Fullerman asks everyone to **STAND UP**

THEN **SIT DOWN**

then **STAND UP** again and check under their shoes for "squashed peas." (This is another sneaky way of making us practice for SPORTS DAY.)

AMY checks her shoes (which are clean). Marcus has pea-free shoes as well. But mine are COVERED in peas.

Marcus says it looks like I squashed a frog,

and then he makes a big deal of moving his chair right away from me. Mr. Fullerman hands me a few paper towels, which get rid of the peas nicely.

Marcus keeps saying YUCK! and making horrible faces.

So I tell Marcus that he's got something GREEN stuck between his teeth that doesn't look so good either. He hasn't, but it shuts him up for a bit.

Mr. Fullerman wants Marcus to MOVE his chair BACK to where it was. And stop being so silly. I agree....

Here's my doodle of Marcus inspired by peas.

(Marcus pea brain)

ENGLISH

Eventually we get the **Squashed** peas under control, and **Mr. Fullerman** hands out **TWO** WORKSHEETS while making us do some extra arm stretches at the same time.

Stretch up!

He says everyone can choose which worksheet to do. Then he STARES at Brad and says,

"Brad, you might like to do worksheet one? And don't forget, I do have eyes in the back of my head."

Which sounds like an odd thing for **Mr. Fullerman** to say.

STOP making faces, Brad.

Until I read worksheet one. (Brad's been rumbled.)

Creative Writing Project 1

Read the beginning of this story carefully. Then I'd like YOU to continue the story on a separate piece of paper. Please write at least one page.

It was clear to Mr. Fullerman that SOMETHING was going on behind his back. He decided the only thing to do was ...

go home.

The end.

If I were going to write an ending for the story on worksheet one, I'd do this. Ha! Ha!

Bit short, I know. Better do worksheet two instead if I don't want to get into trouble (again).

Creative Writing Project 2

I would like you to write your own fable with a similar theme to the fable we read in class, "The Boy Who Cried Wolf." The story can be from your own imagination or based on something that might have happened to you in your own life.

At least one page, please.

This is my version of a FABLE — all based on the family barbecue I was telling Derek about earlier that we had last weekend. Enjoy.

The Boy Who Said,
The Sausages Are Burnt

By Tom Gates

This is the story of a family who wouldn't listen to their **VERY** smart son (that will be me, then). It all began when the **SUN** came out and my dad thought it would be an **EXCELLENT** idea to have a barbecue. I said,

Doesn't it always rain when you get out the grill, Dad?

And he said,

Don't be **daft**. Of course it's **NOT** going to rain!

(Like *THAT'S* never happened before.)

So I watched Dad wheel the grill out
from the corner of the garden.

It was covered with some special protective plastic that Dad told me would keep it

EXTRA clean and ready to use in an instant!

But underneath the "protective plastic" the grill was full of revolting **gunge**.

I told Dad the grill didn't look THAT clean? And Dad said that it just needed a quick brush down and all that BLACK **gunge** would BURN off during cooking.

I said,

Are you sure? It looks really disgusting.

But Dad wasn't listening to me. He was looking at Mom, who was *RUNNING* toward us in a very **BIG PANIC.**

She told Dad,

I've **COMPLETELY** forgotten that Uncle Kevin and Auntie Alice and the cousins are coming to lunch.

Dad said, When? And Mom said, TODAY. Which would have been OK until she added ... In five minutes! Dad said, "Oh, great." (But not in a JOLLY way.) Mom wanted to know how long the barbecue would take? And I said, "It will take FOREVER. It always does."

But Dad said,

> Don't listen to Tom.

And gave me a LOOK.

He ASSURED Mom that he knew EXACTLY what he was doing. "I can just throw on a couple of extra sausages for them."

← Extra sausages

(Without wanting to SPOIL the story, you can probably see what's happening here.)

Dad + NOT listening to me ⇒ = DISASTER

When Uncle Kevin arrived EARLY, Dad was busy telling Mom that EVERYTHING would be fine because he was a

> barbecue expert. ☺

122

And Uncle Kevin said,

HELLO! Did someone say barbecue expert? I'm here!

And Dad whispered, "Great, that's all I need." So Mom suggested that we should leave both the barbecue experts to get on with **BURNING** the lunch.

Which Dad didn't think was very funny.

All this talk of sausages was making me hungry. I really HOPED the barbecue wasn't going to take too long.

Auntie Alice and the cousins were in the kitchen holding a MASSIVE bag of snacks. I told them they should

EAT them NOW

because the barbecue could take AGES. Auntie Alice looked SURPRISED and said,

You're having a barbecue? I thought it was going to rain.

Mom said it would all be fine. (It wouldn't.) Then she asked me to go upstairs and let Delia know that everyone was here. And I said,

What's the point? She won't be pleased to see us.

Which was true.

Get lost.

Mom said, "Just go and knock on her door."

But **I** had a **MUCH** better idea than that.

I showed the cousins how to make some **paper bangers** and how to use them too.

Then we all took them upstairs and stood outside Delia's bedroom door. I think using the paper bangers to let Delia know that everyone was here was a **genius idea!**

Delia came **storming out of** her room and told us to **STOP** being annoying little boys.

So I told Delia that the cousins were NOT little and she was being rude.

Before Delia could get even more grumpy, Mom called upstairs and told us,

The barbecue is nearly ready!

I l**oo**ked out into the garden but all I could see was

THick SMOKE EVERYwhere.

The smoke seemed to be getting **THICKER** and thicker.

Mom had to rush around the whole house closing the windows to stop the **SMOKE** from coming in. I couldn't see Dad at all. I could only hear him calling from the smoke-filled garden for someone to...

Bring me a PLATE QUICKLY!

Turns out Uncle Kevin wasn't much help after all. He'd escaped back to the house because he said the smoke was getting in his eyes and he couldn't stop coughing.

Mom handed me a plate 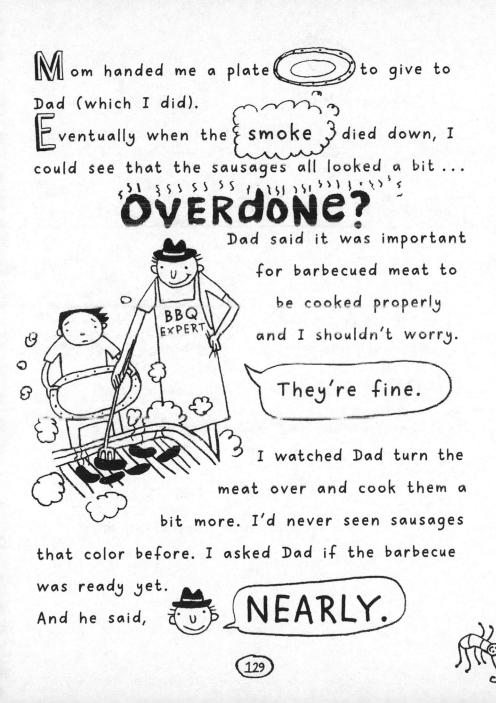 to give to Dad (which I did).

Eventually when the { smoke } died down, I could see that the sausages all looked a bit...

OVERDONE?

Dad said it was important for barbecued meat to be cooked properly and I shouldn't worry.

> They're fine.

I watched Dad turn the meat over and cook them a bit more. I'd never seen sausages that color before. I asked Dad if the barbecue was ready yet.

And he said, > NEARLY.

And I said,

"The sausages look a bit ... **burnt,** Dad?"

And Dad said, "They're not burnt — they're just WELL DONE."

But when he tried to take the sausages

off the barbecue and put them on the plate,

they were ALL

stuck fast

to the nasty black

gunge left on the grill. I reminded

Dad that he said the gunge would

burn off
during cooking. And Dad told me I should go

back to the house and find something more

USEFUL to do.

Tell everyone that lunch is all under control.

(It wasn't.)

I left Dad scraping the sausages up while trying not to make too much of a mess on the plate.

Mom was trying to keep the smoke out of the kitchen with lots of tea-towel wafting. She asked me how everything was going.

I said, OK ... sort of. Which wasn't EXACTLY what Mom wanted to hear.

The cousins had taken my advice and eaten all the snacks.

Empty

SNACKS

BANG

BANG

Now they were playing with their paper bangers again.

I joined in and discovered that if I timed my paper banger SWING just right ...

NOISE

I couldn't hear a word Mom was saying.

"Sorry, Mom?"

BANG!

At least it took my mind off the burnt barbecue lunch that I knew was coming.

FINALLY Dad appeared through the SWIRLING smoke that was still hanging around,

looking very pleased with himself and holding a nice BIG plate of (**burnt**) barbecued food. Well, he WAS holding a plate ... right up until I SWISHED the paper banger over my head and made a SPECTACULARLY LOUD ...

 BANG!

And just when Dad thought that this barbecue couldn't possibly get any worse, it started to RAIN.

A lot.

Uncle Kevin's eyes got better just in time for him to see all the burnt sausages on the ground.

Dad blamed my paper banger *guilty* for making him drop the food, while the cousins kept asking what was for lunch now? *hungry* Uncle Kevin said,

This is one **BIG** barbecue disaster!

Which was true but <u>**not**</u> very helpful (and it really annoyed Dad).

I tried to make a suggestion but everyone was distracted by ROOSTER (Derek's dog).

...ho suddenly JUMPED over the fence and snatched a sausage.

Dad suggested that he could put some more sausages on the barbecue as it was still hot? But Mom wasn't keen on that idea and neither was anyone else. Especially when the cousins pointed out how many ants were everywhere now.

Then Delia appeared and said,

Where's all the food?

Mom pointed to the ground, then to Rooster. Who was eating another sausage.

And THAT'S when I managed to

SAVE THE DAY . . .

by suggesting that maybe

we could get takeout instead?

TAKE OUT

Yes, let's!

Yeah

At last

Whatever

Great idea

Lovely

It was the first time ALL day that anyone had really listened to me.

(Better late than never.)

The end.

Result! →

There, now that's all done.

I'm about to do some more MONSTER doodling

when **M**r. **F**ullerman
SPOTS what I'm up to.

He announces to the class that if we're
finished, we should

"bring up our books to get them graded

straightaway."

I give him my book – and
hope for the best. :)

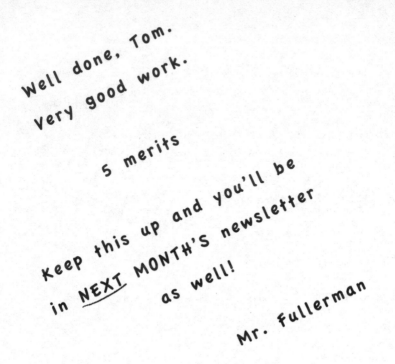

Well done, Tom.
Very good work.

5 merits

Keep this up and you'll be
in <u>NEXT</u> MONTH'S newsletter
as well!

Mr. Fullerman

I'd forgotten about my EXCELLENT
DOODLE book cover being mentioned in the
NEWSLETTER – oh, and with the PHOTO
Mrs. Mumble took too.

I'll have to get a few EXTRA copies and leave them lying around the house so Mom and Dad are reminded about my good work and will say nice stuff to me like

Well done, Tom

while proudly showing off the NEWSLETTER to THE FOSSILS. Who might even give me some extra pocket money for being such a GOOD, hardworking grandson.

You're too kind, Granny.

Then Mom will put the NEWSLETTER on the fridge. (And if she doesn't, I will.) Which will annoy Delia a lot.

I can't wait!

Mr. Fullerman says unfortunately this month's NEWSLETTER won't be ready to take home for a few reasons.

Photo-copier

(a few reasons)

Luckily, I have other things to think about as well as my special mention in the NEWSLETTER. Like:

○ Who'll be picked to be a buddy?

Me?
Maybe?
Maybe not.

○ More genius ideas that annoy Delia.

Guess who I am.

Very funny.

○ The NEW DOGZOMBIES video.

Me, Derek, and Norman want to make our very own MUSIC video for DOGZOMBIES (our BAND). We watch DUDE 3 music videos all the time so thought it would be AMAZING and fun to make our own. We've been talking about it for ages.

Let's do a video.

Derek's dad says he can help us.

Which is OK as long as he doesn't keep trying to butt in (like usual).

He's already been suggesting we watch a few more "classic music videos."

no

no

no

What do you mean you've never seen "Sledgehammer"?

I'm here

While I'm busy thinking of VIDEO ideas, Mr. Fullerman **surprises** me by saying ...

"You too, TOM, ARMS UP!"

Because he keeps making us do EXTRA SPORTS DAY practices when we're least expecting it.

Like now.

It's making it VERY difficult to finish off my LARGE doodle. And Marcus keeps telling Mr. Fullerman when I'm drawing. (He's snitched quite a few times now.) Luckily for me, Marcus has been getting on Mr. Fullerman's nerves too. He tells Marcus to get on with his own work.

Sir

hummph

Which I agree with.

I've had to use ALL the excellent tricks I know to get this doodle finished.

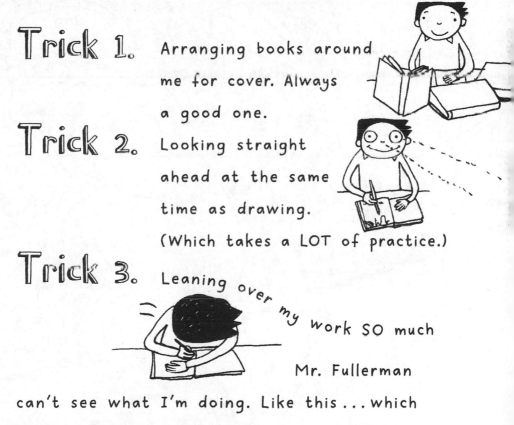

Trick 1. Arranging books around me for cover. Always a good one.

Trick 2. Looking straight ahead at the same time as drawing.

(Which takes a LOT of practice.)

Trick 3. Leaning over my work SO much Mr. Fullerman

can't see what I'm doing. Like this ... which seems to be working. Even Marcus can't see.

Yo!

I'm upside down.

WAFER
TREE

(As it's MATH tomorrow, I'll probably have to
start a new one to keep me going.)

BUDDIES

? **Today** we get to find out about the buddies....

Oh, and there's math too. 🙁

(Doodle ideas ready if I get bored.)

It's not such a big deal if I don't get chosen.

I tell **AMY** she'll definitely get picked. And she says, "I'm not so sure."

So I say, "How can you say that?"

And she says, "Who'd pick me?"

I tell **AMY**, "You wouldn't want to pick an idiot, would you?"

"Thanks, Tom."

Brmmm

Brmmm

It's supposed to be a compliment, but from the way **AMY** said "Thanks, Tom" maybe it didn't sound like one.

Mr. Fullerman is busy handing out letters about who's going to be a buddy and what they have to do.

Becoming a buddy

Being a buddy to some of the younger children is a very responsible role.
All buddies are expected to be helpful, kind, good listeners with good advice.
Your teachers are there to help.
Remember to be the BEST buddy you can be!

Mr. Keen

He tells the whole class, **"If you don't get chosen this time, you will have another chance next term."**

Then he hands a letter to...

 and I say, "Told you!"

And then to ... ME!

Looks like I'm going to be a buddy to some kid in Class 2R?

Let me see who it is.

Joey Dawson.

That name rings a bell.

Marcus hasn't been chosen this time. He's peering over my shoulder to see who I've got.

He says, "Ha! Ha! That kid is trouble." And I say, "Well, I'm going to be a GOOD buddy and keep him out of trouble."

Then I remember who Joey Dawson is.

(I'm sure he's not like that ALL the time?)

Hooray, it's BREAK TIME

I meet up with Derek and Norman, who have both been picked to be buddies. Derek says his buddy seems nice and Norman's buddy looks a bit like him (only smaller).

I can see Joey on the other side of the
school grounds.

He's waving at me. I tell Derek and
Norman that he's my buddy.
"Look, here he comes now."

We all watch Joey walk right through a game
of soccer and not notice a thing. Which
doesn't go down well with the other kids.

I want to make a good buddy impression, so
I say, "Thanks for choosing me as your buddy, Joey!"

Joey smiles but doesn't say anything.
I'm trying to remember what sort of stuff
is in the letter, and what I'm supposed to be
helping Joey with as his buddy.
I add ...
"Got any worries about anything, Joey?"
He shakes his head no.
"Maybe school?"
Joey shakes his head again.
"Friends or teachers giving you a hard time?"
Joey shakes his head.

(This buddy business is going to be easy.)

Then I ask him,
 "Have you got any questions you want to ask me?"

And Joey thinks for a bit ... and says,

"Yes, can I be in your band, please?"

Which takes ALL of us by surprise.

Huh!

I wasn't expecting that question.

So I tell Joey that we're not looking for new band members right now.

"You can come to our next band practice and watch us if you want?"

Joey says, "That would be great."

Then he jumps up and down and punches the air, saying, "YES! YES!" Which is funny!

Until he accidentally

'BiFF'S'

YES

Mr. Fullerman, who's walking past him on break
duty. Mr. Fullerman is NOT very happy because
he's spilled his cup of tea as well.

He tells Joey, **"Joey, you must be more careful!"**

Then he adds, **"Tom, you're his buddy.**
You should be looking out for him."

Like it was my fault! (It wasn't.)

Derek and Norman think it's a BAD idea to let Joey watch our band practice.

"He'll break something," Derek says.

"He's worse than me," Norman adds.

The band could definitely do with a practice and another gig.

The last time we played, it was for Granny Mavis and her Over 70s and Make Group. (Not sure it was a proper gig, though?) I promise Derek and Norman that if Joey turns up, I'll make sure he doesn't touch (or break) anything.

(Don't know how ... but I'll try.)

(Granny's Over 70s Cake & Make)

NEWSLETTER

and other interesting facts

Mr. Keen, our headmaster (or **RED** master, as I call him when he gets **CROSS**), told us in assembly that the NEWSLETTERS have all been posted to our parents now.

"Along with some other important information AND your midterm REPORT CARDS!"

I'm hoping that the GOOD mention in the NEWSLETTER will make up for anything **dodgy** that might be **LURKING** in my REPORT CARD. (Fingers crossed there's no mention of made-up LATE NOTES or that kind of thing.)

Mrs. Nap goes on to tell everybody about the SCHOOL TALENT SHOW AUDITIONS.

She says we are hoping to see "LOTS OF YOU TALENTED CHILDREN ALL COMING ALONG FOR THE AUDITIONS!"

Mrs. Nap explains, "This year's production is a talent show, so anyone can join in. AND there will only be one dress rehearsal once you've been chosen, unlike last year's play."

Which is good to know.

I managed to avoid last year's PLAY—unlike Solid.

(Solid as a tree. He was very good.)

Maybe **DOGZOMBIES** could be part of the show this year, especially with my **NEW GUITAR,** and because **DOGZOMBIES** can now play **SIX** whole songs all the way through.

I can see it now....

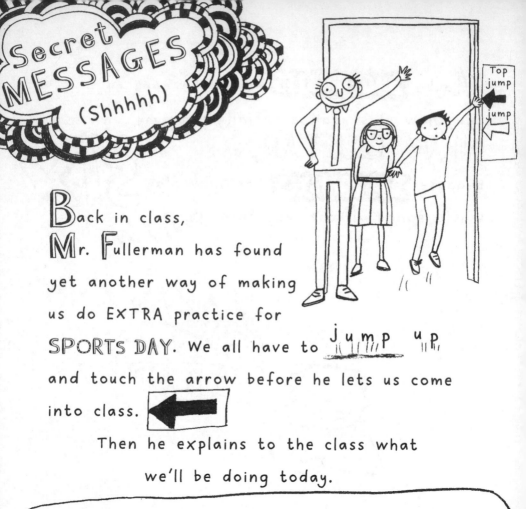

Secret MESSAGES (Shhhhh)

Top jump
jump

Back in class,
Mr. **F**ullerman has found
yet another way of making
us do EXTRA practice for
SPORTs DAY. We all have to Jump up,
and touch the arrow before he lets us come
into class.

Then he explains to the class what
we'll be doing today.

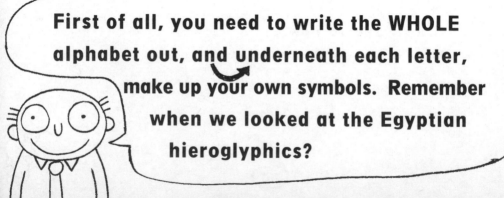

First of all, you need to write the WHOLE alphabet out, and underneath each letter, make up your own symbols. Remember when we looked at the Egyptian hieroglyphics?

That's what I want you all to do.

I thought it sounded a bit dull.

Zzzzzzzz yawn yawn ... I was getting

ready to start a new doodle ...

when Mr. Fullerman gave us some examples

of a SECRET MESSAGE written in code.

We had to work out what the message

said. It was BRILLIANT!

Crack the secret code below, then make up your OWN CODE for the alphabet.

A B C D E F G H I J K
L M N O P Q R S T U V
W X Y Z

Answer: HARD WORK

Next, we have to invent our OWN CODE.
Which could be VERY useful, especially if I
don't want certain people to know what
I'm writing about....

Nosy

? Sniff

Marcus is LO**OO**KING
at what I'm doing and
SNIFFING right by my ear.
I tell him to stop doing both and he says, "I'm
busy concentrating on my own code" (he's not).
His pen has started to leak and it's

leaving ink on his hands, which
he keeps putting on his face.
I try to tell him what he's doing.
But he ignores me and says (Whatever.)
    (I did try.)

I spend the rest of the lesson making up my own

MONSTER ALIEN

code. Which I am VERY pleased with!

Once we've finished making up our own code, Mr. Fullerman wants us to write a letter to the person sitting next to us. I write this one for Marcus, then pass him my ALPHABET so he can work out what it says.

It takes him a while.

Eventually he gets it.

Huh?-

Ha! Ha!

Joey

Buddy duties are proving to be trickier than I first thought. Every SINGLE break time and lunchtime, Joey comes to say

Hello!

But that's ALL he says. (Joey doesn't talk much.) I tried to pass a few tips on about

getting by in Oakfield School.

But it's hard to tell if he's interested or not.

Mr. Fullerman is on break duty (again) and he's looking over in my direction. So I'm trying to show him that I'm being an excellent buddy.

I ask Joey if he'd like to have a game of
soccer with me and a few of my friends,

   "Just a little kick around."
And Joey nods YES.
   So I get a ball and ask Derek
and Solid to join in too. We're
kicking it to each other, nothing fancy.

Joey's actually pretty good at soccer. He's doing
OK. Mr. Fullerman is still wandering around the
school grounds keeping an eye on everyone. And
(hopefully) noticing what a GOOD buddy I'm being.
I kick the ball HIGH in the air and call out,
   "Joey ... on your head!" And Joey jumps up
and tries to HEAD the ball back to me....

Well, I think that's what he wanted to do.

The ball FLIES off his

head in the opposite direction and lands

right in . . . Mr. Fullerman's cup of tea.

Which spills EVERYWHERE (again).

Mr. Fullerman says,
"For GOODNESS' sake, Tom, will you LOOK where you're kicking that ball!"

And I want to shout, "It WASN'T ME!"

But because I am a NICE buddy, I say, "Sorry, sir."

Marcus has been watching us and comes over.

Joey

He says, "I'm glad I don't have a buddy like yours."

And I say, "It was an accident, wasn't it, Joey?"

But Joey's already gone back into school to avoid **M**r. **F**ullerman and me (I think). Marcus says, "I told you your buddy was trouble."

Thanks for that, Marcus.

On the way home from school, Derek gets out **TWO** caramel wafers.

"My buddy gave them to me for being nice." And I'm thinking I DESERVE **LOADS** of WAFERS for [not] snitching on Joey. (Who's been staying out of my way since the soccer incident.)

Derek gives me one of his wafers, which is nice of him. I try to make mine last all the way home by eating it in sections.

Like this:

Break in half

Eat in sections

I'm just finishing the last tiny little bit when I open the front door, go into the kitchen, and find THIS ON THE FRIDGE!

OAKFIELD SCHOOL
NEWSLETTER
ISSUE FOUR

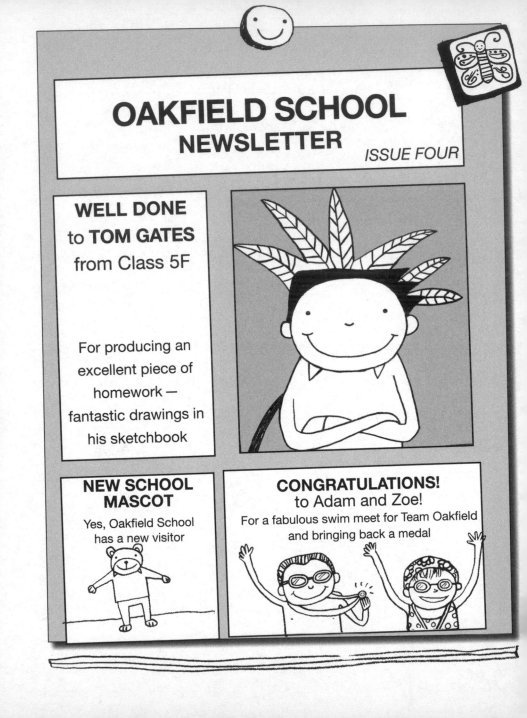

WELL DONE to **TOM GATES** from Class 5F

For producing an excellent piece of homework — fantastic drawings in his sketchbook

NEW SCHOOL MASCOT

Yes, Oakfield School has a new visitor

CONGRATULATIONS!
to Adam and Zoe!

For a fabulous swim meet for Team Oakfield and bringing back a medal

My (HEAD) looks like a GIANT
PINEAPPLE.

(Shame.)

Mom says she is VERY pleased with me. But
we need to have a little (CHAT) about
a few other things when Dad finishes work.

(We do? That doesn't sound good.)

The only time Mom says things like that is if
I'm in trouble or if Delia has been blaming ME
for stuff I didn't do.

Who ate all the jam?

Tom did.

Empty

Who used all the towels?

Tom did.

Delia is upstairs **LURKING** around in the bathroom. I'm going to ask `her` what she's been saying about me **NOW?**

I wait for Delia to come out ...

and when she does, I notice that her hair has turned a VERY odd color. It looks a bit ... green?

It IS **GREEN**!

I follow Delia into her room to get a PROPER look.

But she shuts the door and tells me to

GET LOST!

I ask her through the closed door,

"What happened to your hair, Delia?"

And she tells me to

"Go AWAY, you're annoying."

So I say, "Did you know your hair's **GREEN**?"

Followed by,

"Why the **GREEN** hair?"

Delia says if I don't go away she'll tell Mom that I've been writing my own LATE NOTES. How does she know that?

I go back to my room, and while I'm thinking of excuses in case Mom and Dad ask me about my late note...I have a

GENIUS IDEA

for a song.

Which goes like this...
(As I've written down the words, it seems a shame not to do some nice drawings to go with it?)

GREEN

AGH!

Delia doesn't want to be SEEN

Because her hair has gone bright GREEN.

It looks the color of a LEAF.

Now Mom and Dad will give her GRIEF.

She tried to make her hair look FINE

But now it's gone a shade of LIME.

Delia . . . she can be MEAN.
Delia . . . her hair is GREEN.

GREEN

I go back downstairs (still singing my new song) and Mom wants to know what I'm singing about.

Delia's GREEN hair.

Delia's clean hair?

And I say, No, green hair.

Then Dad comes in from his shed and *CONGRATULATES* me on being in the NEWSLETTER, then adds that we need to talk about a few other things too. So I change the subject quickly and say, "Delia's got green hair."

Just then, **THE FOSSILS** (Granny Mavis and Granddad Bob) `POP` in to say "hello." Like they do. And Granny says, "Who's got **GREEN** hair?"

And I say, "Delia."

Granddad laughs and says, "At least she's got hair, not like me!"

Then I add, Or Dad. Which is true, but Dad doesn't look too happy now.

Mom goes upstairs to see Delia, and Dad says he's off to get changed.

Granny Mavis mentions she's taken up knitting again. She says, "I could make Delia a if she needs one?"

Which is a GREAT idea.

Maybe I should help Granny with a few hat ideas.

Like these:

(This one is my personal favorite.)

Dad suddenly appears wearing ➡

THOSE shorts again.

He tells everyone, "I'm going
for a brisk run." (Like we wanted to know.)

Then Mom comes back downstairs and says
that **D**elia's had a bit of a

HAIR-DYE DISASTER.

I say, "Really? I hadn't noticed." Mom says, "She's
probably been using some **TERRIBLE** cheap
hair dye. Rubbish hair DYE Not like the one **I** use." FAB HAIR DYE

I tell Mom that Granny Mavis has
offered to knit Delia a hat.

"To cover up her green ➡ **HAIR**."

Mom says,

Actually, Delia's quite upset about her hair and doesn't want to see anyone because she's feeling a bit...

And I say, Like a tree?

Mom gives me a **look** and says,

No, Tom, she's feeling a bit self-conscious and embarrassed.

Granny says "Poor Delia," then tells us they're off to the shops to pick up a few odds and ends.

(From the look of Granny's list, it's mostly "odd" things.)

Buy ingredients for
sausage and jam rolls

peach and pea soup

Raspberry & tomato PIE

Then Mom says BYE to **THE FOSSILS** who wish her **LUCK** sorting everything out.

Mom WAS being all nice and sympathetic about Delia's hair.

Poor Delia.

Right up until she discovered it was **HER** hair dye Delia had been using. Now she's really **NOT** happy about that!

FAB HAIR DYE

It's quite late when Dad gets back from his run. He looks RED in the face and is limping a bit. He says,

Puff
Puff

"I'm in agony. I think I've pulled a muscle."

Mom asks, "Is that part of your carefully planned fitness regime too?"

Then she says, "At least you have an excuse not to run in the PARENTS' RACE on Tom's SPORTS DAY."

How did she know about my SPORTS DAY? I've been keeping it quiet. Especially after last year's race.

Dad

Mr. Fingle →

(Last year's race) →

I say, "You don't HAVE to come. My class is always **LAST** anyway."

Dad says he'll be **fine** and he's looking forward to running and **BEATING** Derek's dad this time. (I'm not.)

Mom wants to know if I'm auditioning for the school talent show tomorrow as well? **How** does she know about that?

"I read your NEWSLETTER and your midterm → REPORT CARD too."

Oh! Oh! My report card has arrived.

Dad says, Which reminds me, we want to talk to you about your report card, Tom.

(I'm getting worried now.)

Dad limps over to get it. I can't remember anything **BAD** that I've done (apart from the LATE NOTE and a few other notes too).

Mom and Dad are both looking at me with very serious faces. They say, "**Tom**, we are very `surprised` that ... "

You are an idiot.

"You're doing SO WELL! It's amazing. Well done! Keep it UP!"

WOW! That's a first for me. My report card usually says things like:

Tom does too much chatting/doodling.

Tom doesn't do enough homework/ math.

But [now] on a scale of Idiot to Genius I'm about here.

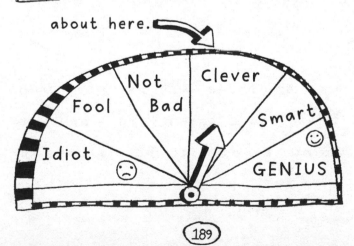

Fool Not Bad Clever

Idiot Smart

GENIUS

om thinks I should put my guitar to good
use and enter **DOGZOMBIES** in
the talent show. "You're doing
so well at everything!"
Good point. Maybe we could do it?

I give Norman a ring first and
then Derek to see if they agree.

Let's!

Yeah.

They do.

While I'm on the phone with Derek, I remind
him about last year's parents' race and how
embarrassing it was watching our dads run.

Then I have a Terrible thought. "Bike shorts... my dad could turn up wearing those bike shorts!"

Derek says,

(Shame.)

While we're chatting on the phone, I can hear Rooster in Derek's garden running around barking like MAD. Derek says Rooster's been chewing all his socks, which is driving him BONKERS. And I suddenly think of an excellent way to avoid a possible SPORTS DAY bike shorts shame after all.

(Genius idea.)

SPORTS DAY!

Now that Dad's bike shorts have miraculously disappeared, I'm fine with him and Mom both coming to my SPORTS DAY.

I'd better remember to bring ALL my own sports kit (for good reason). On the way to school, Derek tells me that his dad has actually been

Wear this

practicing for the parents' race.

He has? Wow, that's embarrassing.

Before we go to the playing field, Mr. Fullerman gives the whole class what he calls a

motivational talk.

His eyes look even **bigger** than usual because he is all enthusiastic.

GO FOR IT, CLASS 5F! TRY YOUR BEST AND HAVE FUN.

I say to **AMY**,
   "**W**hat he really means is ... don't be rubbish and come in last again."

Which is true.

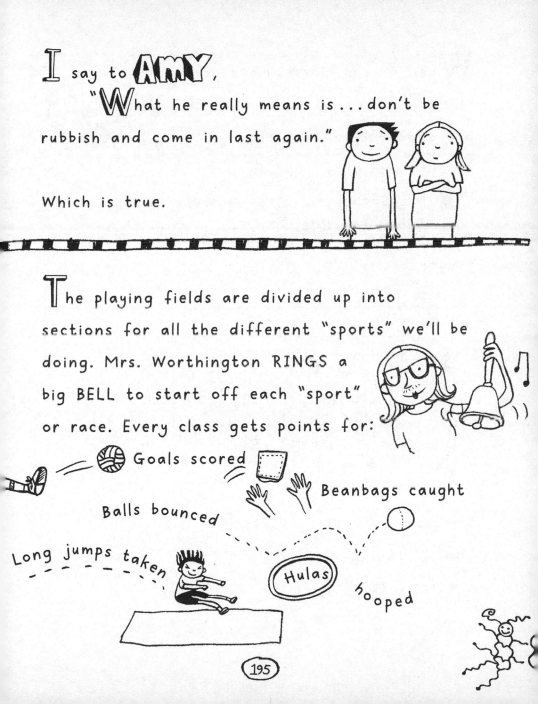

The playing fields are divided up into sections for all the different "sports" we'll be doing. Mrs. Worthington RINGS a big BELL to start off each "sport" or race. Every class gets points for:

Goals scored

Beanbags caught

Balls bounced

Long jumps taken

Hulas hooped

When all the classes have done every "sport," the points are added up and the **WINNERS** are announced—after the parents' race, of course.

Mr. Sprocket's class is wearing shirts with **SLOGANS** so they look like a proper team.

We just look like ... Class 5F.
Mrs. Worthington rings the bell))to begin the first session.

Solid gets us off to a good start with a spectacular Hula-Hoop. Mark Clump and Amber Tulley Green don't do badly either. It's not my favorite "sport," but I manage to add a few points as well.

Go!

((

Solid!

Go, Solid!

Beanbag catching is a disaster.

We're missing them all over the place. Beanbags are flying everywhere! Thankfully, Leroy Lewis and Ross White do a really good job catching theirs for Class 5F.

Marcus is complaining about feeling all "itchy" when he KEEPS on missing the basketball challenge.

And he blames me for *shoving* him, which I did (accidentally).

Mr. Fullerman seems to be smiling, which is better than last year.

Oh, well.

AMY and Indrani are telling Julia that she's doing really well and not to be nervous about the long jump, which is our last sport.

It's not helping that Mr. Sprocket is leading his class in a LOUD . . .

Give me a W
Give me an I
Give me an N
Give me another N
Give me an E
Give me an R
Give me an S

What have you got?

There's a slight pause as none of the class can work out what they've just spelled. In the end it's Mr. Fullerman who says,

"It spells WINNERS, but don't count on it"

to Mr. Sprocket's class.

Mr. Fullerman's **EXTRA** SPORTS DAY training starts paying off, as we're doing very well in the beanbag relay race.

Mr. Keen is wandering around saying encouraging things like:

"Perfect pass, Pansy" and

"Really fast run, Robert."

There are lots of families, friends, and parents on one side of the field behind a barrier who are *cheering* too.

I can't see 👀 anyone from my family ... yet. Mrs. Worthington rings the bell for everyone to stop for:

Drinks, oranges, and BISCUITS

Which is VERY popular. During the break, Mr. Fullerman tells us that everyone is doing BRILLIANTLY and we're definitely NOT going to come in last this year.

Yes! Yes!

(I think he's more pleased than we are.)

Norman has somehow managed to eat **WAY** too many biscuits. And as the sugar starts to kick in, he's rolling around on the ground with his legs in the **air** saying...

Look, I'm a dying fly!

"Yes, you are, Norman."

(Oh, dear.)

The last sport for Class 5F is the long jump. I still can't see any of my family in the crowd at all. Until AMY says,

You're popular.

I glance over to where Amy's looking.

Now I can see...

AND HEAR them.

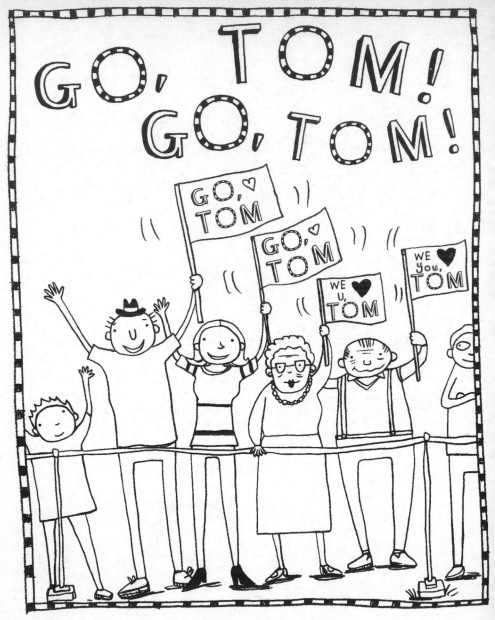

(Shame.)

I manage to get **THE FOSSILS** not to wave the

WE LOVE YOU, TOM banners.

Luckily, I'm not the only one with an embarrassing family. Julia Morton's parents are wearing T-shirts ...

with her FACE on them.

Which hasn't helped her feel any less **NERVOUS.**
Mrs. Worthington rings the bell and says, "*It's time for the last sport. GOOD luck!*"

Oh, NO!

Which is **LONG** JUMP in our case.

I take my turn... *run* as
fast as I can and ...
throw myself into the sandpit.

Yes

It's not a bad j u m p either.
Good enough for THE FOSSILS to take out
the **WE LOVE YOU, TOM** banners again.

Yeah!

WE ♥ U, TOM

WE you, TO

Most of the class has jumped, and there's just TWO kids to go. Mr. Fullerman (who's been having a sneaky peek �",⊃ ⌄,⊃ at the scores) says,

Only a few points between Mr. Sprocket's class and us now.

Which is good news.

The last TWO jumps need to be as LONG as POSSIBLE!

Julia Morton and Marcus say But I'm not sure they're feeling confident. **OK**

Marcus goes first. The class starts clapping to help him jump farther. When he starts running, they all say...

"Whhhhhooooooooooooooooo!"
until he lands.

Then it's an "Oooooooh?" as his long jump is ... only a tiny bit better than last time.

Itchy →

Marcus says he got distracted in midair by his ITCHY T-shirt. (If you say so, Marcus.)

Then Julia goes to jump.

She looks very NERVOUS.

The class goes...

Whhhhhooo

OOOO!

Because Julia's jump is **AMAZING!**
We're all cheering and clapping. But we won't
know who's won the SPORTS DAY trophy
until after the parents' races.
(I'd forgotten about that.)

Just like last year, some dads are taking the race a **LOT** more seriously than others. My dad is trying to pretend the race is

Just a bit of *FUN.*

But from the determined LOOK on his face and the fancy running shoes he's wearing, I can tell he wants to **WIN**.

Mrs. Worthington sets them off with a whistle ⋝ this time.

Fancy shoes

Dad manages to **HUFF** and PUFF himself into...

THIRD PLACE!

(Embarrassing headband)

PUFF

YES!

Ahead of Derek's dad (Mr. Fingle), which he is VERY pleased about.

I say to Derek, "Phew, over for another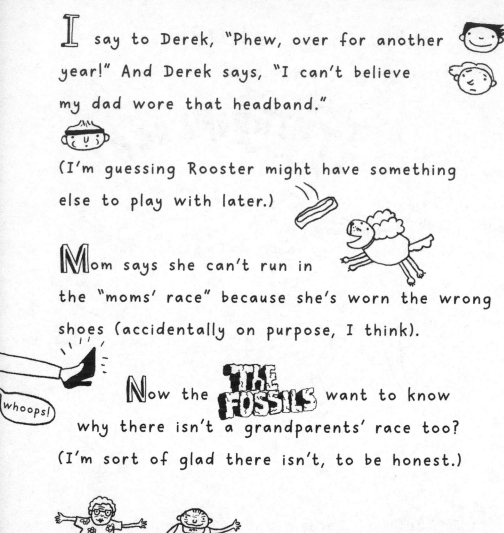
year!" And Derek says, "I can't believe
my dad wore that headband."

(I'm guessing Rooster might have something
else to play with later.)

Mom says she can't run in
the "moms' race" because she's worn the wrong
shoes (accidentally on purpose, I think).

whoops!

Now the **THE FOSSILS** want to know
why there isn't a grandparents' race too?
(I'm sort of glad there isn't, to be honest.)

Mr. Keen comes over and says they have added up ALL the points and are ready to announce the

"winner of this year's SPORTS DAY **Trophy, who is . . .**

Class 5N!"

It's Mrs. Nap's class...and we're SECOND. In front of Mr. Sprocket's class. But from the way Mr. Fullerman is leaping around and

cheering

you'd think it was us who had won.

I've never seen him so happy.

The VERY **best** thing about coming **second** at SPORTS DAY is that **Mr. Fullerman** is in an EXCELLENT mood :) for the rest of the week.

He has made a special SPORTS DAY DISPLAY, which is...

SECOND 5F THIRD 5

Sports Day was won this year by 5N

Everyone who took part had a fantastic time. Especially 5F and Mr. Fullerman.

SECOND WAS CLASS 5F

right outside Mr. Sprocket's classroom.

Sports Day Winners 5N

The morning of the auditions for the school **Talent Show**

I'm a bit achy after **SPORTS DAY.** (All that jumping into sandpits and catching beanbags.)

On the way to school Derek and I discuss the audition and what song we should play. Derek says it

has to be "Smoke on the Water."

And I say, Why's that?

And Derek says, "Because the old folks loved that song and Mrs. Nap and Mr. Sprocket are quite old so they'll like it too."

Good point. ⇨

I've brought my new guitar to school. And I'm a bit nervous that something might happen to it. I get even more worried when the first person we see is...

Joey.

He's not been around much
since the soccer incident.
But because I am a GOOD buddy,
I say, (Hi, Joey) and tell him
we're auditioning for the school talent show.
He says, (I'll see you there.)

He will?

Right away I'm thinking I'll have to keep an EXTRA eye on my guitar. I don't want anything happening to it with Joey around.

In class, I ask **Mr. Fullerman** if he could keep his beady eyes 👀 on my guitar until it's time for the auditions. I don't ask him like THAT.

Obviously.

Please, Mr. Fullerman, could you keep my guitar in a safe place?

AMY, Indrani, and Florence are all singing for their audition. I ask Marcus what he's doing and he says,

"A magic act that I've been practicing a LOT. So it's really good."

And I say, Can you do any magic now?

And he says no because he needs his special box of magic tricks. Which sounds interesting.

I tell Marcus that my granddad taught me how to do a really good

MAGIC TRICK and I can show

him if he wants?

Marcus says,

 "Go on, then ... impress me."

MY GRANDDAD'S MAGIC TRICK

Empty

Granddad's trick goes like this:

1. Take a tissue and **scrunch** it up in your hand, then say

I can make it *disappear*.

2. Then stand up and hold the tissue in your hand. Move your hand up and down while counting to four like this.

One... Two... Three...

Four...

3. Then on the fourth or fifth time, LET GO of the tissue by throwing it behind the person's head so they don't see it.

Now open your hand really slowly to show that the tissue has DISAPPEARED.

It does take a bit of practice.

Gone

But it worked really well on Marcus.

School Talent Show AUDITIONS

Joey comes to our classroom to collect us for our audition because he is helping Mr. Sprocket.

I hold on to my guitar tightly and say, "Hi, Joey." He nods hello.

Ready?

We're walking to the hall when Norman says, "**DUDE 3** is definitely coming to play here, because the whole school is talking about it."

And I say, "I hope it's **TRUE**, Norman. It would be **SO** good."

(Rumors often start in school that aren't true.)

Aliens have landed in the playground.

Really?

Rumor in school

Frisbee →

What really happened

Derek is already waiting for us along with Marcus (who's auditioning next).

Marcus is wearing ... a **CAPE.**

He's swishing it around and trying to be all dramatic.

Mr. Sprocket calls out,

DOGZOMBIES NEXT, PLEASE.

But before we can start, Mr. Sprocket asks for help

carrying some chairs and checking the drum kit is at the right height first, please.

We have no choice.

Just prop your guitar over there for a second, Tom.

I'm NOT going to do THAT! So Joey offers to hold it. And I have to stop myself from saying,

NO WAY!

Then MARCUS says, I'll look after it. Which is only a tiny bit better than Joey, but I don't have much of a choice. So while we go with Mr. Sprocket to pick up the chairs and a few music stands, Marcus is left holding my guitar. Like this ... ➡

I can see 👀 him FIDDLING with the strings! I tell him, "Don't touch the strings." But he ignores me. Now he's TWIDDLING with the end of my guitar and doing ROCK STAR poses while pretending to play it. I can't take my guitar back FAST enough!

Marcus says, "Don't snatch."
Guitar in hand—we get ready for our audition.

Hello—we're DOGZOMBIES.

But when I start to play "SMOKE ON THE WATER," it doesn't sound like "Smoke on the Water." It sounds TERRIBLE.

My guitar has gone out of tune because Marcus was fiddling SO MUCH with the strings. I have to keep going.

But it's a rotten audition. I can tell from the faces Mr. Sprocket and Mrs. Nap are making. They look like they're in pain.

When we've finished, Mr. Sprocket says,

Well done. Just a few tuning issues to be sorted out ... but not bad, boys.

Which is better than I thought. Derek tells me not to worry. Norman says, It wasn't so bad.

Marcus says, "What happened? You were RUBBISH! More like DOG'S DINNER than DOGZOMBIES."

Which is irritating ... but true. Derek says, "Thanks, Marcus. Let's see how YOU do, then?" Marcus SWISHES his cape and goes off to perform.

He announces himself as *"MAGIC☆ MARCUS."

Which sounds like MAGIC MARKERS ⌁and makes us all LAUGH. Ha! Ha! Ha!

Marcus is doing tricks with cards and all kinds of different things and is surprisingly good, which is a bit annoying.

Now Joey has brought along AMY, Florence, and Indrani for their audition.

"How did you do?" Amy asks me.

I was about to say, "Not bad" or "OK, but might have done better" when Joey decides to **BUTT** in and tells AMY.

They were TERRIBLE, all out of tune.

Thanks, Joey! He's normally quiet. Some buddy he turned out to be. It wasn't my fault the guitar went out of tune.

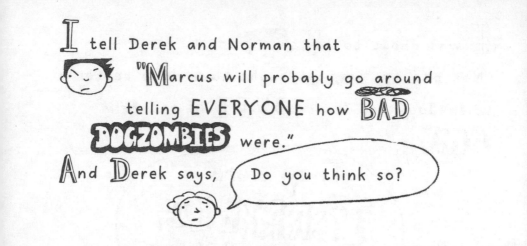

I tell Derek and Norman that "Marcus will probably go around telling EVERYONE how BAD DOGZOMBIES were."

And Derek says, Do you think so?

Yes, that's EXACTLY what Marcus does.

Hopeless, they were.

Shame.

DOGZOMBIES were RUBBISH.

Oh, dear.

It was painful to listen to.

Now ALL the school is talking about DUDE3 playing at the school talent show. AND

the RUBBISH audition DOGZOMBIES did.

Which was THE WORST audition EVER in the WHOLE

HISTORY of the school.

(That last bit's not true ... but that's what it FEELS like everyone is saying.)

It's [not] very long before the list of successful AUDITIONS gets pinned up on the school notice board. Somehow ... **DOGZOMBIES** has made it.

Oakfield School Talent Show Audition Results

If your name is below, you're in the SHOW!
We'll have ONE dress rehearsal before the show.

Well done, EVERYONE

Brad Galloway

Julia Morton

Minnie Verner

June Rawlings

Tom Gates

Norman Watson

Derek Fingle

Marcus Meldrew

Amy Porter

Indrani Hindle

Florence Mitchell

Paul Rogers

Jenny Chan

Christina Brown

Roger Wood

Emily Border

Chad Dury

Paul Jolly

SPECIAL GUEST APPEARANCE TO BE ANNOUNCED

In fact, looking at the list, I think **everyone** who auditioned made it.

Right at the bottom it says
SPECIAL GUEST APPEARANCE
to be announced.
Which looks interesting?

Could the RUMORS be true after all?

Family Outing to the MOVIES

On the way home we **BUMP** into Joey going the other way.

(When I say we bumped into him... I mean we **BUMPED** into him.)

I ask him if he's **OK?**

He nods. Then he says,

When can I come to your band practice?

I'd forgotten about that.

And I'm looking at Derek, who seems a bit alarmed.

I tell Joey that we're SUPPOSED to be filming our BAND VIDEO soon.

It might not be a good time to come and watch us. Sorry.

Joey says,

I could come and help you and bring WAFERS.

And Derek shrugs his shoulders like it's OK with him. So I say, "OK, Joey, it'll be at Derek's house. I'll let you know when."
Joey says, "Yeah, thanks." Then he runs off and bumps into someone else coming around the corner.

AGH! Whoops

When I get home 🏠 **M**om reminds me that we're supposed to be having some

QUALITY family time together tonight.

And I say, We are?

"Yes, we're going to the movies. We have to go somewhere dark or **D**elia won't come with us while her hair's still a bit **GREEN**."

"**W**hat are we seeing?"

Mom says it's a **great** movie that's had **lots** of good reviews.

"It's called **The** **tter**."

And I say, What's it about? Because I've [never] heard of the movie? Then Delia butts in and she says,

It's about an OTTER, stupid.

So I say, "Not necessarily, it could be a movie about SPIES and 'THE OTTER' is a code name for a secret agent."

And Delia says, "OR it could be about an OTTER and that's why there's a MASSIVE picture on the movie poster of AN OTTER."

The OTTER

Mom says, "All right, Delia, that's enough."

Then I suggest that if Delia doesn't want to be seen with her GREEN hair, she could always ask Granny Mavis to knit one of these hats for her?

Like this

or this→

Then Dad comes in and says,

Has anyone seen my bike shorts? I can't find them anywhere.

This seems like a good time to disappear to my room and wait until we're all ready to go.

Which takes **AGES**.

WAIT! I forgot my glasses!

We're so late we nearly miss the start of the movie. As we're buying the tickets, Mom is getting **STRESSED** because she likes to sit near the ➞ **FRONT** of the theater and she's worried it will all be **FULL**. And she **HATES** it when people eat too **LOUDLY**. Mom thinks there should be **RULES** for what you can eat in the theater.

Crunch

Munch

Slurp

I've brought a few fruit chews that I unwrap BEFORE the movie starts. Otherwise Mom will keep STARING and nudging me until I stop.

We all manage to get seats near the front before the movie starts. Delia has got her hood up and looks even grumpier than usual. I tell Dad that I don't want to sit next to her if she's taking

Grump
→

off her sunglasses again.

So Dad sits between us.

We're all settled and the lights are just going down. Mom's happy with her seat. There's no one eating too LOUDLY near us. Everything is great. When this happens to me....

I can't see a thing now!

That's just great. I keep moving from side to side but I still can't see the movie. Mom tells me to stop fidgeting, Tom.

SWAPPED

I say, "I can't see." So Mom swaps seats with me. And for about a minute I can see the whole screen.

Then the **TALLEST** man in the world with the ← **BIGGEST** head does this ... and that's when I realize who's sitting in front of me.

It's Solid and HIS DAD.

I tap him on the back and say, "Hi!" And Mom says, "Shhhhhhh."

I decide to go and sit next to him because I can't see anything behind him or his dad.

The movie is REALLY Funny. Even Delia is laughing (but I'm not going to look at her without her glasses again).

Mom keeps tapping me on the head every time Solid and I chat. Even a tiny bit.

Solid says, "Is your whole family here?"

And I whisper,

 "Yes, we're having quality family time watching a movie. So we don't have to talk to each other."

 Then Mom Taps me on the head again and tells me to ...

 Shhhhhhhhhh ...

Groan.

When the movie is finished, Dad says he's going to the toilet and he'll meet us outside. We all get up to leave and Solid and I are chatting about the movie, our SPORTS DAY, and the school auditions, STUFF like that.

It's only when he says BYE and walks off with his dad that I realize how similar they both are.

Solid

His dad

Mom wants to know what's taking Dad so long and she goes off to find him, leaving me outside with Delia (who's getting grumpier).

Then suddenly Delia *Huh!* notices that Ed, her old boyfriend, is coming out of the theater with some of his friends. She tells me, "Don't move or ELSE." And ducks behind me.

I decide to have some fun and start moving from side to side so Delia has to follow me. I can hear Delia whispering behind me, "Don't you DARE" as Ed looks up and sees me. I wave and say, "Hi, Ed, fancy seeing you here."

Ed comes over and says, "Hi, Tom." And I say, "Good movie, wasn't it?" and he says, "Great ... are you still in your band?"

249

$\mathbb{A}$nd I say, "Yes, thanks."

Delia's still crouched down with her hood covering her GREEN hair and she's trying to sneak away without Ed noticing. Which might have worked if I hadn't moved out of the way at exactly the same time as a

BIG gust of wind *SWEEPS* Delia's hood right off her head.

Delia's **GREEN** hair stands out a LOT.

Everyone is looking at her —including Ed. **M**om and **D**ad come back just in time to stop Delia from taking her **REVENGE** on me. She says, "You wait."

Which doesn't sound good.

So I suggest Delia lighten up and have some **FUN.** "Like me!" Mom says it's nice that we're both enjoying ourselves. (Well, I am.... Delia looks a bit grumpy and **GREEN** still.)

Missing :Homework

With all the stuff that's been going on in school, it's easy to forget about my...

Homework?

Because **M**r. **F**ullerman is STILL in a super good mood from **SPORTS DAY**, he says I can bring it in tomorrow. Which is good news for me.

I've been spending **LOADS** of my time at home (and in class) PLANNING and thinking of ideas for the **DOGZOMBIES** VIDEO.

Planning for the video

WILD Thing Video

There are SO many things we could do. Like:
- Make **WILD THING** masks.
- Make WILD THING posters to put in the background.
- Film in the garden, which looks a bit jungley in parts.

WILD THING

I've got LOADS of IDEAS going on in my head. And writing a WHOLE page about "MY SPORTS DAY" just isn't one of them.

"**T**omorrow" has come around a bit **too** quickly — I've only managed to write a bit of my homework while on the way to school this morning.

I have to finish it off under my desk ... and on my lap ... so **M**r. **F**ullerman can't see what I'm doing.

Under the circumstances I think I've done OK?

My Sports Day
By TOM GATES

I REALLY LIKED SPORTS DAY THIS YEAR BECAUSE WE NEARLY WON! YEAH! AND MR. FULLERMAN HAS BEEN IN A GOOD MOOD.

WE HAD NICE ORANGE BISCUITS, WHICH WAS A TREAT. YEAH!

Tom,

Y o u   s   e   e   m

t   o   b   e

s   p   a   c   i   n   g

o   u   t   your words a lot?

This does not fool me into thinking
you have done a whole page!

Don't try this again.

Mr. Fullerman

Phew ... could have been worse.
No detention or mention of "EXTRA WORK."

DOGZOMBIES VIDEO

After an EXHAUSTING week at school, me, Norman, and Derek are very busy making some important decisions about the **DOGZOMBIES** video that we're filming today.

1. Hats or no hats?

2. Sunglasses or no sunglasses?

3. Outside or inside?

4. Masks or no masks?

5. Wafers now or later? Cool!

Wafers later is the only decision we've made so far. Mostly because we don't want Norman to peak too soon.

I say, "What do you think **DUDE 3** would do if they were making this **video?**" Derek says he doesn't think they'd wear masks.

It's a good point. We stick to the **DOGZOMBIES** T-shirts instead and film inside Derek's garage, as it looks like it might rain. Mr. Fingle has offered to help out and has set up the camera on his fancy TRIpod. Which is great. But it does mean we can't move around much or we won't be in the shot.

$\mathbb{D}$erek's dad starts talking about

classic music videos of our time.

AGAIN.

So Derek has to remind him that we're just doing this for fun. We're saved when Mr. Fingle's phone rings, which keeps him busy for a bit. Derek says, "Shall we just press play on the camera and have a go then?"

It's a good plan. But we can't work out who's going to do it, because it's tricky pressing play, then running back into the shot. We're just about to start filming when this time MRS. Fingle comes in! She says, "You have a visitor to see **DOGZOMBIES**!" We do?

"Hello."

It's Joey.

Who I invited to watch us do a band practice ...and then forgot all about.

"Come around tomorrow."

"Ok."

Joey says his mom will be picking him up in two hours.

And Derek says,

"TWO HOURS!"

like it's a really, really long time. Then Joey shows us a very small cool camera that his mom has lent him to use today. "I can do some filming too if you want?"

Which is an **excellent** idea. (Joey's turning out to be really helpful after all.)

Though Joey does *knock* the tripod over twice.

Mr. Fingle comes back and starts making a few filming suggestions.
Some are better than others....

But it does make TWO HOURS WHIZZ by.

Joey's mom turns up just as we're really

Joey's mom →

getting into filming. She says,
"This looks good! I'll help you put
the video together if you want."

Norman says, "**SWEET**."

(He means that's good.)

Then Joey says, "That reminds me—I brought
you these."

He throws me a whole pack of

caramel WAFERS!

YEAH! Then knocks over the camera for the THIRD time.

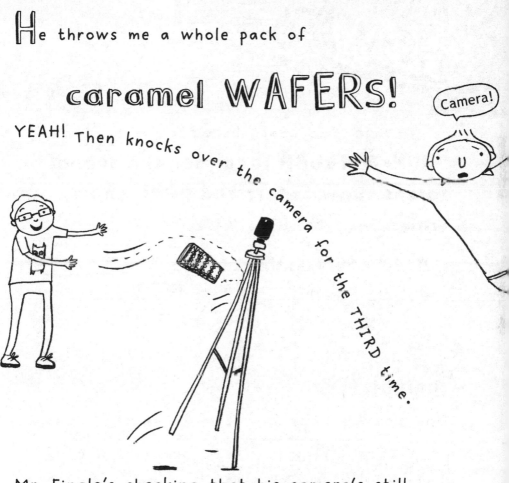

Camera!

Mr. Fingle's checking that his camera's still working (it is). I'm thinking Joey has turned out to be an excellent buddy after all.

Bye!

TALENT SHOW → rehearsal

Mr. Fullerman reminds us that there's a

"RUN-THROUGH today for the school talent show before the REAL show, which is ... tonight."

I whisper to **AMY,** Tonight! Is he sure?

And Mr. Fullerman says, **"Yes, Tom, tonight."**

How could I have forgotten when the school production was?

TALENT SHOW is **THIS** THURSDAY. DON'T FORGET!

SCHOOL NOTICE BOARD

TALENT

TALENT SHOW TONIGHT Special Guests

The GOOD news is DOGZOMBIES' rehearsal time is at 11:15. It looks like I'll be missing ... MATH. ☺

Result! (Making the DOGZOMBIES video was a bit of extra practice for us too, which is good.)

Marcus has his run-through before us at eleven o'clock. He's sitting next to me complaining (as usual). He thinks he should be on last. And I say, "How do you work that one out, Marcus?" and he says, "Because my act is the best one." And I say, "It might not be?"

And he says, "No one else is doing magic tricks like me."

And I say, "What about the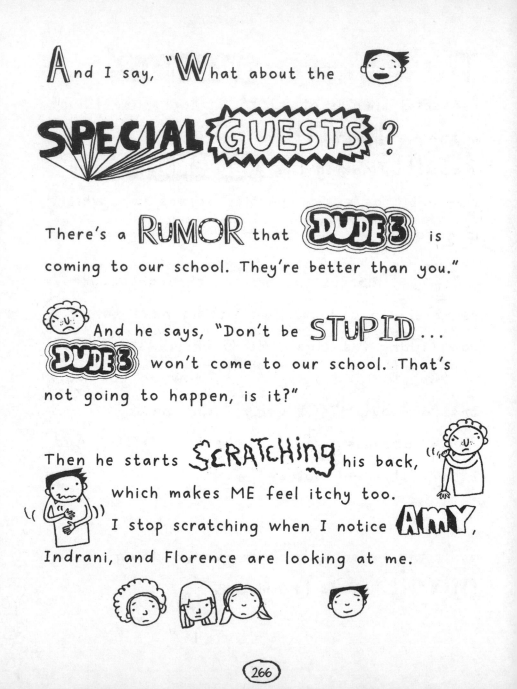

SPECIAL GUESTS?

There's a RUMOR that DUDE 3 is coming to our school. They're better than you."

And he says, "Don't be STUPID... DUDE 3 won't come to our school. That's not going to happen, is it?"

Then he starts SCRATCHING his back, which makes ME feel itchy too. I stop scratching when I notice AMY, Indrani, and Florence are looking at me.

They are getting ready to sing after **DOGZOMBIES**,
followed by Mark Clump.

Who apparently is
bringing in one of his **pets**
that he's trained to do tricks.

(Maybe his snake? Which would be impressive.)
Brad is doing street dancing (not behind
Mr. Fullerman's back this time either).
I *wish* I knew who the
SPECIAL GUESTS were!

If it's NOT **DUDE 3** ...who can it be?
Mr. Sprocket and Mrs. Nap are not saying a
word at the run-through.

They tell me,
"You'll have to wait and see like everyone else, Tom."
Which is irritating. Because I wanted to go home and tell Delia that

DUDE3 is coming to our concert tonight.

She's not going out much because of her (slightly) GREEN hair.
But it would still annoy her to miss them.
And I would remind her how she'd missed them ... a lot.
Ha!
Oh, well ...it can't be DUDE3, can it?
Norman MUST have got that wrong.

At lunchtime Joey comes to find me and he says he's got a finished film of us playing

"WILD, THING."

"I'll ask my mom to send it to you. It's really good."

(I am a GENIUS for getting Joey as a buddy. OK, I know he picked me, but it's still worked out well.)

High five

$\mathbb{B}$ecause of the school production,
everybody is allowed to go home an
hour earlier to get ready.

$\mathbb{W}$hich doesn't take me and Derek long
to do.

BEFORE

AFTER

$\mathbb{D}$erek is at my house and we're looking at
some copies of **ROCK WEEKLY** when
I suggest that if we're going to look more
like a **ROCK** band, "I should wear
some shades

or **SPIKE** up my hair...like this?"

And he says, "Do you think so?"
It might be a good idea.

I go into the bathroom and
help myself to some hair gel
that's been there for a while.
I think Uncle Kevin bought
it as a present for Dad...as
a **joke.**

I still have a selection
of Delia's
sunglasses that we can
"borrow" for tonight, which both Derek and I
think we look pretty good in.

Derek stays at my house for some dinner,
and while we're eating, Dad comes in holding a
plastic bag. He says, "I've got myself some
new shorts for running."

Which he's pleased about.

I whisper to Derek,
"Let's hope Rooster's still hungry."
Which makes him laugh.

TALENT → **SHOW TONIGHT**

(PLUS SPECIAL GUESTS!)

.Chat

Chat

All the kids that are performing tonight are getting ready in the classrooms near the hall. There's a **lot** of excited chatting going on before the show starts. Me, Derek, and Norman are all wearing our **DOGZOMBIES** T-shirts.

I show Norman the hair gel and say, "I think I should spike up my hair to look cooler and more like a

ROCK STAR"

And **AMY**, who's with Florence, hears me and says, "You should do it, Tom! That would look really good!" Norman just says,

YEAH!

because he's already getting a bit twitchy (like he does).

So I get a big handful of hair gel and put it in my hair, where it stays in a big

BLOB.

Derek says, "I think you need to rub it in a bit."

Which I do. "What now?"

AMY and Florence are looking at my hair. Florence says, "Maybe you should spike it up using a brush?" But I don't have one. **AMY** says I can borrow her brush, which is nice of her. Now that I've got half a

TON

of hair gel in my hair, I must look a bit silly.

Derek suggests I

go and find a mirror so you can see what you're doing.

(Good thinking.) I head to the toilet and try to SPIKE up my hair using **AMY**'s funny little round brush.

I've never used one of these before.

I twiddle it around the front of my hair, then try to drag it up^{ward} into a **SPIKE**.

But it's **STUCK**. So I twist it around a bit more. Which doesn't work at all. This is NOT good. I'm trying not to **PANIC**. But the more I twist the brush, the more tangled up it gets.

This is turning out to be a

DISASTER!

I'm taking so long that Derek comes to find me.
He says, "We need to get ready now, Tom." And I say, "There's a tiny bit of a problem."
And Derek says, "I know, Mr. Sprocket wants us to go on early because of Marcus."

I don't think Derek has realized that the brush I'm holding in my hand is actually STUCK. I keep trying to get the brush out while asking,

"What's the problem with Marcus?"

Derek says, "Mr. Sprocket wants us to perform **FIRST** because Marcus has got—"

I say,

"Nervous? Cold feet?

More annoying than ever?"

Derek says,

"No, not quite. He's canceled because he's got . . ."

"A bit of a **RASH**..."

(Marcus scratching.)

Derek tells me his mom called and said it's
not serious, but Marcus says he can't do his
tricks because he's all ITCHY.

itchy →

(Marcus on
SPORTS DAY)

That explains a lot.

Finally, Derek notices the brush sticking out
of the top of my hair.
"What's wrong with your hair, Tom?"
"The brush is stuck,"
I say.

Derek has a go at trying to pull the
brush out. I say "AGHHHH!"
so he stops.

"How did you do THAT?"
"I twisted the brush and now it's stuck ... the hair gel made it worse."

I need to get help ... �FAST!
But no one knows what to do.

Not even Mr. Sprocket or Mrs. Nap can get the brush out of my hair.

Mrs. Mumble comes over. She says, "Joey got a comb stuck JUST like that."

"**H**ow did you get the comb out, Mrs. Mumble?"

Mrs. Mumble makes a scissor-cutting

movement with her fingers.

"His mom had to cut the comb out.

It was the only way, I'm afraid."

That's just great, then. GROAN...

    Mr. Sprocket says that we can go

on later if I need the time to sort out the

brush.

I say, "YES—we need LOADS more time."

(Like a WEEK.)

Mr. Sprocket says I will have to get my mom

or dad to help now. Derek says he could go

to look for my mom in the audience if I

want.

"They should be here by now?"

Reluctantly, I say OK.

Mom takes one look at me and the brush and says, "How did you manage to do **that**, Tom?" I say, "It's a mystery. I just brushed my hair." (I don't mention the half ⎹ton⎸ of hair gel.)

AMY is feeling a bit guilty because it was her idea to use the brush.

She says, "I don't need it back if you have to **BREAK** it."

I really hope Mom's not going to do THAT!

Kiai!

But the only pair of scissors that anyone can find to cut my hair with are a bit **BLUNT**, with round tips that are meant for paper.

 Mom says, "I CAN'T use those, Tom."

So I have to either:

o   Ignore the brush (bit tricky).

o   Wear a BIG hat.

o   Wear a mask.

I don't want to go onstage with this brush **BOUNCING** around on my head.

The TALENT show has already started and seems to be going OK without Marcus.

Mr. Keen made an announcement that there might be a few changes to the running order of the show.

We're now going to play LAST, so I'm hoping my hairbrush problem will be ALL sorted by then.

But it's not looking good.

Ta-da!

Norman and Derek are shaking their heads and staring at me.

"This isn't working, is it, Tom?" Derek says.

He's right.

I don't want to go and play "**WILD THING**" in front of the school with a BRUSH sticking out of my hair.

I tell Mr. Sprocket and Mrs. Nap that I'm REALLY sorry, but I won't be able to play now.

"Never mind, Tom, We'll get the **SPECIAL GUESTS** to go on earlier," Mrs. Nap says.

I'm thinking this could actually turn out to be really **GREAT**, because Mrs. Nap knows I'm a **DUDE 3** fan. I ask her, "Is **DUDE 3** coming to play, then?" and she says, "That would be telling!"

Which probably means NO.

Mom goes back to her seat to watch the rest of the show (even though I'm not playing anymore). She says she'll deal with the brush when I get home. (Shame.)

At least I get to watch the other talent-show performances that I didn't see before.

Like Mark Clump and his talking budgie.

F lorence, **AMY**, and Indrani singing.

(They're really good!)

Brad Galloway's **EXCELLENT** dancing.
Some little kids each doing
a line from a poem
(which takes a bit of time).

A few more singers.

And **A**ctors.

And a **V**entriloquist.

(My favorite so far.)

When the last performance is over, Mr. Keen comes on and all the lights go down.

He says it's been a wonderful show with SO many talented children from Oakfield School.

"I'm sure you're all wondering who Clap **the SPECIAL GUESTS are tonight?"**

Clap

Clap   Clap   **YEsssssssss!**

"Well, we are VERY privileged to welcome a WORLD-FAMOUS band to our school for a one-off performance — for the very first and possibly the LAST time."

And I'm looking at Derek and Norman, who've come to see who it is as well.

Norman says, Told you **DUDE3** was coming.

But I can't see them anywhere. Then Mr. Keen says,

"We need to give a BIG OAKFIELD SCHOOL WELCOME to the one and only ..."

(Drum rolIIIIIIIIIIIIIIIIIIIII...keep rolIIIIinggggggggggg...)

"YOU3!"

And for a split second I think Mr. Keen has

said and I'm jumping up and

down and cheering when I see ...

Leather trousers

Mr. Fullerman, Mr. Sprocket, and Mrs. Worthingtash, dressed like they're going to ride motorbikes.
Mrs. Worthington has on a FALSE MUSTACHE (well, I hope it's false).
Me, Norman, and Derek look SHOCKED.
Like this ...

They start singing ...

Get your lesson ready
Head out to the classroom
Get the children running
Practicing for SPORTs DAY

We're a NEW teachers' band
Who are born to be MILD
We can keep our cool
In Oakfield School

BORN TO BE MILD.

BORN TO BE MILD.

It's a funny song ... some of the adults are LAUGHING extra hard!
Mr. Sprocket and Mr. Fullerman are stomping around pretending to be **ROCK** stars. But it's MRS. WORTHINGTON who's going CRAZY!

I say to Derek, "This is the MADDEST thing ever!" It might not be DUDE3, but **You3** are so hilarious I almost forget about the brush stuck in my hair.

Then the WHOLE school claps and Cheers when they finish playing.

CLAP! Hooray CLAP! Hooray

295

I think the kids in our school will be talking about this teachers' performance

FOREvER!

Thank you and good night.

Now that the show's over I say bye to everyone and go to meet up with Mom and Dad, who both think the teachers' band was "VERY good!" Dad says, "Makes me want to be in a band!"

Mom gives him a look 👀 and says, "I don't think so."

(I agree with Mom.)

At least Dad has brought the car so I don't have to walk home with this ⟍⟍⟍⟍ brush sticking out of my hair. (Which is a relief.)

I can avoid people STARING at me, wondering what I've done. I can't avoid Delia, though. When we get home, Mom and Dad are even telling Delia how FUNNY the teachers' band was.

Delia isn't listening. She's too busy looking at me and shaking her head.

She says,

"How did you do that, idiot?"

So I say, "It was an accident — a bit like your **GREEN** hair. Mom's going to help sort it out now."

But before I get the chance to think about what Mom is ACTUALLY going to do (CUT the brush out), she suddenly appears with some scissors

and does this ...
SNIP! SNIP!

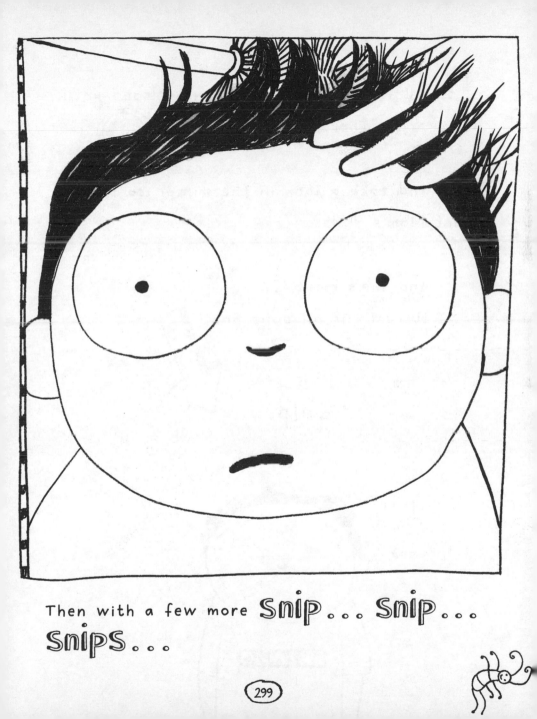

Then with a few more **Snip**... **Snip**... **Snips**...

It's all finished. I keep my eyes closed until Mom says, "There, all gone now."

I go and take a look in the mirror to see what Mom's done.

And she's right ...
It really is all gone now.

Gulp.

Delia catches me looking at my hair. I'm just waiting for her to say something HORRID as usual when she says,

"Don't worry, it will grow back ... eventually."
Which isn't the *worst* thing she could have said, I suppose?

I go upstairs to get ready for bed, then remember to let Derek know the important news—I do a quick doodle and put it up at my window.

NEWS FLASH

THE HAIRBRUSH IS GONE

(and so is some of my hair).

Mom and Dad both come in to say good night. They tell me my hair looks very cool shorter. (I'm not so sure.)

 I think it looks a bit odd?

So I'm lying in bed, sort of going to sleep. But I can't stop thinking about:

1. **YOU3**-so funny!

2. My CHOPPED-off hair.

If I have to sit next to Marcus (when he stops itching and comes back to school) with my hair like this, he'll probably just keep making stupid jokes all the time.

Which will drive me

BONKERS.

Did you cut your hair
with a knife and fork?

Hair today,
gone tomorrow.

Then all of a sudden, I get one of MY
VERY BEST-ever ideas that comes to
me in a FLASH.

I jump out of bed quickly and grab
a comb.

Until my hair grows back a bit more, I could just do this?

Let's see if it works...

ANOTHER...

GENIUS IDEA

If I do say so myself.

(Thank you, thank you.)

How to make a PAPER BANGER

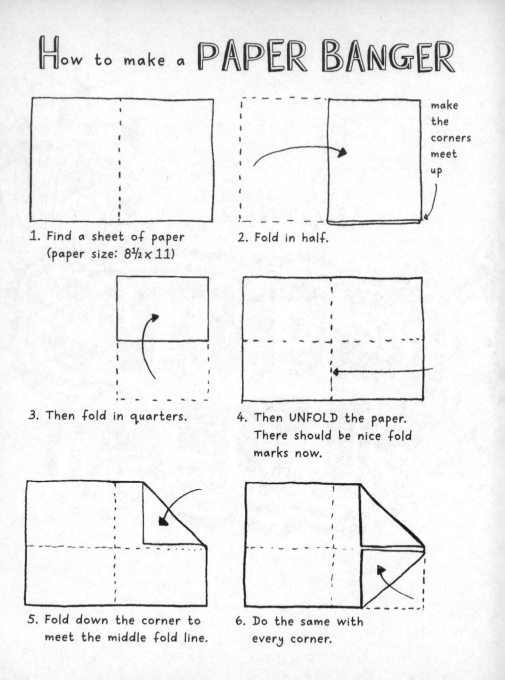

make
the
corners
meet
up

1. Find a sheet of paper (paper size: 8½ x 11)

2. Fold in half.

3. Then fold in quarters.

4. Then UNFOLD the paper. There should be nice fold marks now.

5. Fold down the corner to meet the middle fold line.

6. Do the same with every corner.

7.

8. Your paper should look like this.

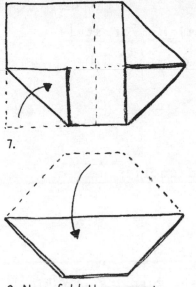

9. Now fold the paper in half, with the flaps inside.

10. Fold the right corner to the middle.

11. Then repeat on the other side.

12. Fold the whole banger in half, hold the corners marked, then flick it down HARD.

Air catches under here to make a BANG!

BANG!

Tom Gates' Glossary

(Which means explanations for stuff
that might sound a bit ODD.)

Yum!

← Biscuits = cookies.

Caramel wafers: Excellent biscuits (cookies) covered in chocolate with layers of caramel and wafer inside.

Crisps: Chips.

Dodgy ≝ something that's a bit ODD or wrong. Maybe slightly peculiar or not quite right. For instance: That apple looks a bit Dodgy. That monster looks a bit dodgy.

←(worm)

Fruit chews ≝ candy.

Garden is a YARD.

Headmaster is a principal.

Mr. Keen

Lessons ≝ the same as CLASSES.

Mate = Friend.

MERITS are special POINTS or STARS awarded by your teacher for excellent work.

Rubbish

Garbage

(or something not very good)

Sports/
P.E. Kit

Gym
Clothes

Tea towels ≡ dish towels.

TELEVISION

Trousers is another word for PANTS.

When Liz was little, she loved to draw, paint, and make things. Her mom used to say she was very good at making a mess (which is still true today!).

She kept drawing and went to art school, where she earned a degree in graphic design. She worked as a designer and art director in the music industry, and her freelance work has appeared on a wide variety of products.

Liz is the author-illustrator of several picture books. Tom Gates is the first series of books she has written and illustrated for older children. They have won several prestigious awards, including the Roald Dahl Funny Prize, the Waterstones Children's Book Prize, and the Blue Peter Book Award. The books have been translated into forty-three languages worldwide. Liz works in a nice cozy shed in her yard and lives in (mostly) sunny Brighton with her husband and three (not so little anymore) children. She doesn't have a pet but she does have lots of squirrels in the yard that eat everything in sight (including her tulip bulbs, which is annoying).